Reviews of the *Birdwatcher's Mystery* series
by Christine Goff

"Very entertaining. Birders and nature lovers alike will enjoy this new twist on the cozy mystery." —*The Mystery Reader*

"You don't have to be a bird lover to fall in love with Christine Goff's charming Birdwatcher's Mysteries." —Tony Hillerman, *New York Times* bestselling author of the *Navajo* mystery series.

"The birds of the Rocky Mountains will warm the binoculars of birders who have waited a lifetime to see real stories about birds in a popular novel." —*Birding Business* magazine

"Christine Goff's Birdwatcher's mysteries are engaging." —*Mystery Scene*

"A wonderfully clever, charming, and addictive series." —David Morrell, *New York Times* bestselling author of *Murder as a Fine Art*

and ... *Death of a Songbird*

"A most absorbing mystery." —Virginia H. Kingsolver, *Birding* magazine

and ... *A Rant Of Ravens*

"Everything you expect from a good mystery—a smart detective and a plot that takes some surprising twists...a terrific debut!" —Margaret Coel, NYT bestselling author of the *Wind River Mystery* series.

"*A Rant of Ravens* is a deft and marvelous debut mystery set in the complex and colorful world of bird-watching." —Earlene Fowler, national best-selling author of *Seven Sisters*

"*A Rant of Ravens* stars a gutsy heroine in fast-paced action with a chill-a-minute finale...enchant nature...A fine-feathered debut." — Carolyn Hart, award-winning author of the *Death on Demand* and *Henrie O* mysteries.

D0199173

A Parliament of Owls

The Birdwatcher Mystery Series

Christine Goff

ASTOR
+BLUE
EDITIONS

A PARLIAMENT OF OWLS

Copyright © 2015 Christine Goff

Typography © Astor + Blue Editions

The right of Christine Goff to be identified as the author of this
work has been asserted.

This Edition Published by:

Astor + Blue Editions LLC, 1441 Broadway, Suite 5015,

New York, NY 10018, U.S.A.

www.astorandblue.com

Publisher's Cataloging-In-Publication Data

GOFF, CHRISTINE. A PARLIAMENT OF OWLS

ISBN: 978-1-941286-62-3 (Paperback)

ISBN: 978-1-941286-64-7 (ePdf)

ISBN: 978-1-941286-63-0 (ePub)

ISBN: 978-1-681200-06-4 (Mobi)

1. Mystery—Thriller—Fiction. 2. Murder Mystery—Fiction
3. Cozy mystery—Fiction 4. Mid-life—Mystery—Fiction
5. Birdwatchers—Fiction 6. Women & Family—Fiction
7. Colorado 8. Title

A catalogue record for this book is available from the Library
of Congress and the British Library.

Cover Design: Didier Meresse, Kate Murphy

This is a fictional work and all characters are drawn from the author's imagination.
Any resemblance or similarities to persons either living or dead are
entirely coincidental.

Dedicated to the amazing Colorado birders on the CoBirds list, who helped me pick just the right owls.

Acknowledgments

Several people helped me by providing technical information for this story. My deepest thanks to: David Lucas, Project Leader of the Rocky Mountain Arsenal National Wildlife Refuge Complex. He is the head of law enforcement on the refuge, and any resemblance to any of my law enforcement characters is purely coincidental. David helped me understand the complex relationship between the various entities that might be involved in solving a crime on the Refuge. If I got it wrong, it's on me.

I would also like to give a shout out to the staff of the Visitors Center. They spent lots of time walking me around the exhibits and answering my myriad of questions.

Additional thanks to my fellow writers and friends. To my RMFW and RMMWA buddies, you know who you are; to the members of my critique group: Marlene Henderson, Laurie Walcott, Chris Jorgensen, Suzanne Proulx, Bruce Most, Tom Farrell, Mike McClanahan, Piers Peterson and Jedeane Macdonald; and to Robert Astle, who wanted me to write about owls.

Finally, thanks to Peter Rubie, who has been a huge support this year; my family for their unconditional love; and my new publisher, Astor + Blue Editions, who is committed to keeping the Birdwatcher's Mystery series circulating. I can think of no better partners than David Lane, Robert Astle, and Jillian Ports to help me navigate the waters of today's publishing world.

Author's Notes

In *A Parliament of Owls*, I have brought back Angela Dimato, the US Fish & Wildlife Special Agent from *Death Takes a Gander*. In *A Parliament of Owls,* Angela finds herself reassigned to the National Eagle and Wildlife Property Repositories, located on the Rocky Mountain Arsenal Refuge in Commerce City, Colorado.

The Refuge offered an interesting setting for a variety of reasons. Originally it was inhabited by bands of Native Americans that roamed the land following the herds of bison. In the 1860s, homesteaders moved in and put down roots. Then, in 1942, the Army expropriated the property to build a munitions plant in the heart of the U.S. Later a Super Fund site, the Arsenal was designated a Wildlife Refuge in 1992—primarily due to a pair of nesting bald eagles.

Located just northeast of Denver, Colorado, the Refuge comprises 15,000 acres of prairie, wetland and woodland habitat. It is home to over 330 species of mammals, birds, reptiles, amphibians, and fish. In the spring, you can see Bullock's orioles, warblers, finches, and other migrating songbirds, and the prairie dog pups and bison calves are plentiful. In the summer the prairie blooms and the burrowing owls come in to raise their youngplus it's a great time to fish. In the fall, the coyotes are well-camouflaged, the mule and white-tailed deer bucks show off their antlers, and the Refuge lakes provide a haven for migrating water fowl. Then, in the winter, numerous bald eagles come to roost, along with ferruginous hawks and other raptors looking to pick off an easy meal against the blanket of snow that covers the grass.

But, in spite of its idyllic setting and aggressive conservation efforts, there are other important things at play on the Refuge. In the United States, it is illegal for any individual to possess a bald or golden eagle or its parts without proper authorization. Located on the Refuge, the

National Eagle Repository provides a central location for the receipt and storage of bald and golden eagles parts and their distribution to Native Americans and Alaskan Natives, enrolled in federally recognized tribes, for use in religious ceremonies.

This comes into play, as well as the conservation issues on protecting other wildlife, as Angela finds herself face to face with death with only A Parliament of Owls to bear witness.

Introduction

Growing up in a small mountain town in Colorado, my father and I fed the hummingbirds. He identified them as broad-tailed hummingbirds, though years later I learned there are actually four different hummingbirds that are common migrants or summer residents of Colorado. It was years after that when my husband taught me to stand very still with my hand outstretched under the feeder to let the hummingbirds perch on my fingers to eat.

As a child growing up in the Rockies, I watched ouzels bob for food along the shore while I was fishing, stood open-mouthed as a red-tailed hawk caught dinner among the wildflowers just beyond camp. Spending summers with my grandmother in Maine, I loved watching the antics of the herring gulls diving for tidbits behind the lobster boats and marveled at the puffin colony on Eastern Egg Rock.

Is it any wonder that years later, when I decided to try my hand at writing mystery novels, I found myself time and again coming back to stories with environmental themes involving birds? At that time, having been a backyard birdwatcher all my life, I could identify all the birds that clambered to my feeders—51 different species. But it was in doing research for my novels that I discovered the bigger world of birding beyond my backyard.

Birders come in all shapes and sizes and with a huge diversity in knowledge. While some birdwatchers just enjoy looking at birds, others want to know the unique characteristics that determine the breakdown of species and subspecies. While some delight in just spotting a bird in the trees, others are only content when they can hear its call. While some thrill at the sight of a robin, others are only interested in the bird they can add to their life list.

To expand my knowledge of birding, I decided the first thing to do was to sign up for a birding trip. The next one coming up happened to be The Rio Grande Valley Birding Festival in Harlingen, TX. My first outing: a canoe trip down the Rio Grande with what turned out to be fifteen world class birders from all over the U.S. and Europe. Sixteen of us pushed off—fifteen seeking life birds (a bird they'd never seen before) and me, for which nearly every bird was a life bird. I remember my canoe mate even teaching me the proper way to use my brand new binoculars.

After that, I was hooked. Since then I have gone on at least two birding trips a year, and birded in nearly every state in the U.S., Canada, Mexico, the Caribbean, Europe, Eastern Europe and Israel. Yet I would still dub myself an intermediate birder, at best. I'm good at spotting the birds, slow at identifying them, and hopeless at birding by ear. Still, I'm continually fascinated by the stories I hear and the things I've learned through watching birds and talking with other birders. I've discovered that the issues affecting birds have global themes relating to the environment and driven by things that resonate with all of us—money, land, love, pride, and power.

It was with this basic understanding I set out to write the Birdwatcher's Mystery series—a group of funny, sometimes serious mystery stories populated with birdwatchers ranging from the amateur to the professional. A Rant of Ravens explores the illegal trading of peregrine falcons to the Middle East; Death of a Songbird looks at the coffee industry and its effects on migratory songbirds; A Nest in the Ashes considers the impact of prescribed burns on wildlife; Death Takes a Gander explores the reasons for a die-off of Canada geese; A Sacrifice of Buntings compares the basic nature of the painted bunting and the keynote speakers at a birding conventions; and, A Parliament of Owls, the newest in the series, looks at the human impact on endangered species.

Mostly, I hope I've presented these important themes in a manner that is accessible and entertaining for everyone, from the novice to the expert, and that gets people thinking about the world they live in.

Happy birdwatching and happy reading!

Chapter 1

Angela Dimato saw the crowd waiting for her in front of the Rocky Mountain Arsenal's Visitor Center and briefly considered turning around. She counted several adults and at least a dozen grade-schoolers, ages eight to ten. Not exactly her idea of a fun morning of birding. It's not that she didn't like kids, she just hated being outnumbered.

Swinging the truck into a VIP parking spot, she cut the motor and reached for her duty belt. She might be playing tour guide this morning, but she was still a U. S. Fish and Wildlife Special Agent and she still planned to carry her gun. She cinched on the belt and checked to make sure her holster was secured.

Through the passenger window, she caught sight of her boss, Wayne Canon, walking toward her and waving. "Good, you're here," he called out. "I brought some gear over for the kids and their teachers. They're ready to go."

Angela climbed out of the truck and tucked a birding guide into her back pocket. "You owe me, Canon."

"Trust me, I know," Wayne said. As the Special Agent in Charge of Law Enforcement for USFW's Region 6, he'd also been acting Project Director for the Rocky Mountain Arsenal National Wildlife Refuge Complex for the past month. The complex was a group of three national wildlife refuges along the Front Range, and Wayne was in over his head. Over worked and under staffed, he had pulled Angela out of the field and assigned her to the National Eagle and Wildlife Property Repositories. Now he was having her babysit.

Initially, the move to the repository had rubbed her the wrong way. She'd taken it as an indictment of her abilities as an agent, like when she'd been reassigned to cover the fishing tournament in Elk Park immediately following Ian's murder. Blaming herself for his death seemed like punishment enough. She was supposed to have been his backup, and he might still be alive if she'd gotten out to the lake more quickly. The images of him swinging in the bird-banding nets still haunted her. But she was a good agent, and she wanted to be, deserved to be out in the field.

Then she found she liked working the repository. She liked working alone, performing forensic investigations on crimes involving wildlife. She felt like she was helping to make a dent in the $23 billion illegal wildlife product industry.

But leading a Monday-morning summer school class on a birding tour of the Refuge...that fell way outside of her purview.

"You owe me big time," she said, reaching back behind the seat for her binoculars and spotting scope.

Wayne glanced over his shoulder at the group and lowered his voice. "I wouldn't have asked you to cover if I had anyone else. I have two agents out and our usual go-to called in sick. I'll make it up to you, Dimato. I promise."

Famous last words, but it was a chit she intended to collect on.

Angela's gaze swept the sun-drenched prairie. In the distance, the Continental Divide cut a purple swatch across the clear blue sky, beckoning with the promise of cooler temperatures. At 7:30 a.m., it had already climbed to seventy-two degrees on the plains and promised to be one of the hottest July days on record.

"I'll bet you that your 'go-to' girl got up and went to the mountains," Angela said.

"Yeah, well, she's going to up and get hers before it's all said and done." Wayne took the scope from Angela's hand and gestured for her to follow. "Come on, I'll introduce you to Tammy Crawford. She's the group leader."

Angela dogged his heels, sizing Crawford up as they approached. Contrasting the schoolteacher's tank top, cotton shorts, and lace-up tennis shoes against her own short-sleeved rough-duty shirt, long pants, and sturdy boots, Angela determined they were exact opposites. Crawford was tall, buxom, and fair, with a smile that made fifty percent of her young charges swoon. Short, with the dark complexion and padding of her ancestry, Angela figured, for these kids, her biggest draw was her gun.

"I'm so pleased to meet you, Agent Dimato," Crawford said, thrusting out a hand. "Wayne was just telling us how lucky we are that you're the one who's going to be showing us around."

Angela's resolve to dislike Crawford thawed under the wattage of the teacher's smile, and she found herself smiling back. "Canon told me you're interested in having the kids see some birds."

"And to learn something about the Arsenal. I teach biology, but my colleague, Mr. Burton, teaches history." Crawford gestured toward an older gentleman, who was attempting to corral a trio of rambunctious boys. "We run the summer school program at Commerce City Academy."

Angela shot a glance at Wayne. That explained a lot. Maintaining positive relationships with Commerce City was high on the Refuge's to-do list. No wonder he wanted someone knowledgeable leading the tour.

Since 1992, when the Rocky Mountain Arsenal National Wildlife Refuge Act was signed, USFW had struggled to maintain a good working relationship with Commerce City. The city wanted more land. The Refuge countered by offering more use. It fit with the primary stated objectives of the Refuge Act, to restore and manage the land, provide a quality wildlife habitat, and implement environmental education programs for urban school children. They'd had already annexed over 917 acres to Commerce City.

As much as she wanted to hate what they'd done with the land, Angela had to admit that the development of Dick's Sporting Goods Park was a feather in everyone's cap. The public-private partnership between Commerce City and Kroenke Sports & Entertainment had resulted in the development of brand new city offices for Commerce City, lots of retail outlets, offices for the U.S. Fish and Wildlife Service, and a new Vistors Center for the Rocky Mountain Arsenal Wildlife Refuge. It also included the world's largest and most state-of-the-art soccer complex in the world, and just a mere 9 miles from downtown Denver.

Kroenke had spared no expense. They had spent $131 million dollars in construction. Amenities included twenty loge-style luxury suites, a unique open concourse design allowing 360-degree views of the fields, and a FIFA regulation-size grass field with an innovative underground heating and draining system. People came, and they came to visit the Refuge, too.

Commerce City Academy was the newest additionthe crown jewel in the city's new educational program. It mattered.

"I leave you in good hands," Canon said.

When he was done saying his goodbyes and had walked away, Angela turned to Crawford. There was no point in putting things off. "I suggest we get started. Why don't you gather the troops and we'll head inside."

While Crawford and Burton rounded up the children, Angela unlocked the Visitors Center and flipped on the lights. The Center didn't officially open for another hour, which left plenty of time for a private tour of the facilities interpretive display.

Waiting for the kids to line up at the door, Angela's thoughts flashed to her late-partner, Ian. This was definitely his bailiwick. Whenever they'd conducted tours, Ian had taken point. He'd been great with children. She remembered asking him once what he would have been if he couldn't be a USFW agent and he'd told her he thought he might like to teach. Maybe today she could channel his spirit.

"We'll start in here," Angela said, leading the kids inside and gesturing for them to sit in a semi-circle on the floor of the lobby. Then she pointed to the circle of exhibits behind her. The dioramas and displays detailed the early times on the plains, the history of the Refuge, and provided animal visuals and hands-on exhibits. One of the boys she'd seen Burton struggle with earlier made a face.

"Do we have to look at a lame museum?"

"Leroy, be quiet," Burton said.

Crawford smiled. "Continue, Agent Dimato."

Leroy wasn't that easy to dissuade. "But you said we were going to spend the day outside."

Crawford looked at the boy. "Didn't Mr. Burton ask you to be quiet?"

"Yes, Ma'am."

"Then be quiet." Crawford beamed at Angela. "Go ahead, Agent."

Speaking in front of a group had never been easy for her, and a group of nine year-olds was no exception. Situations like this made her insides tremble. That's why Ian had always taken the lead. Angela tried to think of where he would start.

"There are some cool things to learn about the Rocky Mountain Arsenal," she finally said. "It wasn't always a wildlife refuge."

"What was it?" asked a girl with strawberry blond braids.

"It started out as short-grass prairie, when large herds of bison roamed the plains." Angela pointed at a stuffed bison marking the exhibit entrance. "American Indians followed the herds, hunting and living off the land. Later, settlers moved west and homesteaded the land, growing crops and grazing cattle. Then, during World War II, the U.S. Army moved in, kicked off the homesteaders and built a chemical weapons manufacturing facility called the Rocky Mountain Arsenal."

"What do you mean by chemical weapons?" Leroy asked.

Angela forced a smile. At least she had his attention. "The government made bombs here. They filled them with mustard gas, nerve agents and napalm."

"What's mustard gas?" asked the girl with the braids.

"What's napalm? Leroy asked.

Angela found herself at a loss. How graphic of a description she was allowed to give? Fortunately, before she could answer, Burton stepped in.

"They're weapons that have killed a lot of people," he said.

The answer seemed to satisfy the kids, so Angela continued. "Eventually the war ended and the plant was demilitarized."

"What's that mean?" asked another girl.

"The army shut down the operations," Burton interjected.

The kids all nodded.

Angela stared out at the faces and chose her next words carefully. "Because the chemicals they used to make the bombs were harmful, the Arsenal was named a Superfund site in the 1980s."

"What's a Superfund site?"

Crawford jumped in. "That's enough, Leroy! Let Agent Dimato

finish."

Angela tried smiling again. Good thing she wasn't being graded. "It's a site with abandoned hazardous materials that's been marked for cleanup. Designating it a Superfund site gives the Environmental Protection Agency, the EPA, the right to come in and monitor the process."

"Hazardous, like the mustard gas?" Leroy asked.

Angela nodded. "The EPA makes sure that immediate action is taken. They get the community involved, enforce the laws against the responsible parties, and ensure long-term protection against hazards. The Arsenal was named a Superfund site in 1987."

"When did it become a National Wildlife Refuge?" Burton asked.

"1992. It's comprised of 17,000 acres, making it one of the largest urban wildlife refuges in the country."

Crawford looked out at the kids. "Does anyone have any questions for Agent Dimato?"

A volley of hands shot up.

"Is that a real gun?" Leroy asked.

"Yes," Angela said. She knew it was her most interesting feature.

"Any questions about the Refuge," Crawford clarified.

"Did they get everything cleaned up?" Leroy asked.

"You've already asked a question," Burton said. "Anybody else?"

It was a good question, so Angela answered it. "They completed the cleanup in 2010."

"What did it cost?" asked a boy beside Leroy.

Odd question from a fourth grader.

As if she could read Angela's thought, Crawford chimed in. "His father's an accountant."

"$2.1 billion," Angela said.

The kid started to open his mouth again, but Crawford showed him her palm and nodded at a girl with large dark eyes. "Amanda?"

"What kinds of animals live here?"

"Great question," Angela said, relieved to be back in more familiar territory. She had always been more about science and less about math. More hands-on and less reporting. "Bison, mule deer, white-tailed deer, coyotes, prairie dogs and rabbits. Plus we have over 300 species of birds."

"What's a species?" Leroy blurted out.

Angela sighed, already feeling exhausted.

"Types," Burton said.

"Are there any dangerous animals?" Amanda asked.

"All wild animals can be dangerous," Crawford said, looking expectantly at Angela.

Angela grinned. This was the best part of her spiel. "The most dangerous creature on the Refuge isn't an animal. It's a reptile—the Western diamondback rattlesnake." Angela was pleased to see one or two of the kids' mouths drop open. Deciding to wrap things up there, Angela gestured toward the exhibits. "I'll be happy to answer more questions later, but right now I'm going to give you about twenty minutes to look around."

Before the words cleared her mouth, the kids were up and streaming past her with Burton close on their heels.

"Thank you, Agent Dimato," Crawford said, standing and dusting off the front of her shorts.

"No problem," Angela said. "Look, I need to make sure we have everything we need on the bus. Can you just make sure that the kids don't touch anything they're not supposed to? We especially don't want them climbing on the stuffed bison." She inclined her head toward the entrance to the exhibits, where one of Leroy's buddies was boosting him onto the back of the large, stuffed mammal.

Crawford moved quickly. "Leroy Henderson, you come down from there."

Thirty minutes later, after everyone had taken a cursory look at the exhibits and used the bathrooms, Angela locked up the Visitors Center. The kids and teachers were once more gathered beside the bus. The temperature had spiked to eighty degrees.

"Okay, listen up. It's getting hot and we need to hurry if we want to see any animals." Angela said, walking over to a large wastebasket near the front of the vehicle. "Since birders need the right tools, I'm going to loan each of you a set of binoculars."

"All right!" hollered Leroy. He tried grabbing at the pair in her hands but Angela lifted them out of his reach.

"Just chill," she said, then immediately felt bad when all of his friends laughed. "Come here, you can help me demonstrate how to use them."

With Leroy as a guinea pig, she showed the others how to set the focus.

"That's so cool," Leroy said, sweeping the binoculars toward the prairie.

Angela grinned. The kid was smart.

"Okay, everyone take a pair of the binoculars and get on the bus," Crawford said. "You can finish adjusting them while we're moving.""

Five minutes later, the kids were outfitted and in their seats. Angela climbed aboard and stood in the front near the driver.

"Before we head out, we need to cover some ground rules," she said. "We're going to drive into the Refuge and stop in the bison pasture. We are not getting out. Bison are big, dangerous animals. Got it?"

The kids all answered in the affirmative. Burton and Crawford nodded.

"Rule number two."

"What was rule number one?" Leroy whispered to his friend.

Angela gave him a dirty look. Just when she was starting to like the kid, he had to come up with a smart ass question.

"Stay on the bus," she said. "You're allowed to get off, only when I tell you."

"Got it," Leroy said.

"Rule number two, keep your eyes open for wildlife. Never shout at them or try to feed them anything. Remember, we are visitors on their land. But feel free to point them out to each other."

"Got it," the kids said in unison. The chatter rose to ear shattering levels until Crawford raised her hand.

Angela nodded her thanks. "After we're through the bison pasture, we'll head out to one of the best viewing sites of our premier prairie dog town. We'll get out there and see if we can spot any burrowing owls."

Leroy frowned. "Why do owls live—?"

"Bison first," Angela interrupted. "Then I'll tell you about the owls."

"Whatever."

It bothered her that she'd lost his attention, but there were fourteen other kids and two adults on this tour to consider. "When we're done looking at the burrowing owls, we'll head to the eagle watch." The platform for watching the roosting eagles in the winter and the nesting pair in the spring was only opened to visitors on special days or for private tours. This year, the kids were in for a treat. "We have two fledglings—baby eagles. And since it's nearing the middle of July, the eaglets are about to leave the nest and fly for the first time. With any luck, maybe we'll see it happen."

Again the kids broke into an excited chatter. Crawford banged on a seat back rail to quiet them down. "Let's listen to Agent Dimato."

Once the noise subsided, Angela continued. "After we're done there, if we have time, we'll head back to the Lake Mary Loop trail and go for a hike."

Leroy's mouth started to open and Angela silenced him by raising her hand. "Rule number three. When we are not on the bus, you need to pick a buddy and stick together."

One of the boys rolled his eyes.

"Remember what I said about the snakes?" Angela said.

The kids grew quiet.

"Do what I say and you'll be safe. Got it?"

Amanda looked as if she was about to cry. Crawford smiled reassuringly, reached forward in her seat, and patted the child on the shoulder. "Does everyone understand the rules?"

The children nodded, chose partners, and then busied themselves practicing with their binoculars. Angela was pleased to see Leroy helping. Maybe his attention hadn't strayed so far after all. Plus there seemed to be more good than bad in the boy, provided his energy was channeled correctly.

Angela conducted a head count and came up with fifteen. Then she signaled the driver. The bus lurched forward. "Okay, everyone, you'll want to get your cameras ready if you have them."

Fifteen phones came out of pockets.

About thirty bison waited for them inside the pasture. After everyone had taken pictures and asked their questions, Angela told the driver to head for E. 72nd and Buckley Road. "Once we get there, stop about a quarter of a mile shy of the intersection." It was off the normal visitors' route, but it would give them the best chance for seeing the burrowing owls.

"Okay, everyone." Angela called for attention, standing and holding onto the bar near the driver as the bus lumbered along the service roads. "We have a huge prairie dog population on the Refuge. They currently live on about 11,000 of our 17,000 acres, while we want them to live on about 2,500 acres. That's why we're working on establishing specific prairie dog towns. We're going to stop at one of the largest designated areas."

"Why don't you guys like prairie dogs?" asked the girl with the braids.

"Because they carry the plague," Leroy answered.

"Yeah," said his friend.

Angela glanced at the boys. "That's not really true," she said. "There hasn't been a case of plague found in prairie dogs in the Refuge since 2002."

"My mom says the prairie dogs have fleas that carry communicable diseases," Leroy said.

Angela looked at Crawford, who promptly took charge. "Leroy, your mom is worried about something that hasn't happened, yet."

"But she—"

"Please continue, Agent Dimato," Crawford said, placing her hand on his arm and dazzling them all with her smile. Subject closed.

Angela turned to the girl who had asked the question. "We do like the prairie dogs, but we don't like it when they build tunnels and mounds and eat all the prairie grass. It makes the land uninhabitable for other wildlife. We're hoping to even things out by reducing the population."

The girl frowned. "How do you do that?"

Angela decided she shouldn't tell her that they shot or poisoned them. Better to put some spin on the facts. "There is one great thing about having lots of prairie dogs. It means we have lots of abandoned prairie dog holes, which means homes for the burrowing owls."

The girl's face brightened.

"Do any of you know anything about burrowing owls?" Angela asked.

"They're funny to watch," said one of the boys.

Angela nodded. "And naturally curious." Which is what made them one of her favorite birds. Active day and night, they loved to come out to see who was visiting. "What else do you know about burrowing owls?"

"They have really long legs and short tails," said a blond-haired girl.

"That's right," Angela said. "Anything else?" She looked around. "No? Well, unlike most owls, their ears aren't tufted. They kind of look like a mini-football on stilts."

The kids giggled.

"Does anyone know how to tell the male and females apart?"

"The males are bigger," answered one of the boys.

"Good guess, but no," Angela said. "Anyone else?"

"The females feed the babies," said one of the girls.

"Another good guess," Angela said. "And it plays a big part in why you can tell them apart. The male and female burrowing owls are actually the same size, but the female spends more time on the nest. That means less time in the sun."

"So the boy birds are suntanned," Leroy said.

"Nope. The males' feathers get bleached out by the sun, so they're actually lighter in color—sometimes," Angela qualified. "Here's another fun fact. Did you know that if you get too near their burrow, the owls can make a sound like a rattlesnake?"

"Are there real rattlesnakes out here?" Amanda asked.

Angela turned to the child. "Yes, but we're not likely to see one. Snakes don't like people. So unless you corner one, they'll move on and leave you alone."

From the girl's expression, Angela wasn't sure she'd made her feel any better. Time for more distraction.

"Who can tell me what burrowing owls use to line their nests?" Angela asked.

Everyone, including Crawford and Burton, shrugged.

"What?" Leroy asked.

"Animal dung," Angela said.

"Poop?" Leroy punched his seatmate.

"Exactly. It keeps the babies warm," Angela said.

"Gross!" The kids erupted into chatter. Amanda giggled. A few moments later, the bus stopped.

Angela issued another warning about keeping the noise down before letting them off the bus. "Keep your eyes open. The owls prefer abandoned prairie dog nests, so they can usually be found on the edges of the town."

"I see one," shouted a girl.

An owl? Angela stooped to see out the window. A prairie dog stood at attention. All of the kids squealed and rushed to that side of the bus, except Leroy. He moved in Angela's direction.

"Inside voices!" Crawford shouted, clapping her hands. The kids quieted down.

"Let's go." Leroy pushed past Angela and bounded down the steps. Angela caught up to him at the edge of the road. Lifting her binoculars, she scanned the edges of the prairie dog town.

"There." Angela pointed to the far eastside of the field. "Think of it like a clock. You're standing on six and straight ahead is twelve. Now back off to the left. There are some owls situated at ten o'clock."

The kids trained their binoculars in the direction she pointed.

"I see them," Leroy cried out.

Angela set up the scope for a close-up view and let the kids take turns looking at the birds while she continued scanning the outer edges of the prairie dog town through her binoculars. When she reached the western boundary, two o'clock on her imaginary timepiece, she tightened her focus. It looked like someone was kneeling near one of the burrows, straight east of the eagle's roost.

"Let me see that," Angela said, commandeering the scope. No visitors were allowed in this section of the Refuge, but through the telescopic lens she could clearly see someone about three hundred yards away at the edge of the field.

"What is it?" Leroy asked.

"Stay here," Angela ordered. "I'll be right back."

Leaving Crawford and Burton in charge of the kids, Angela took out across the field. She could feel her adrenalin pumping as she closed in for a confrontation. Whatever this person thought they were doing, they were going to cease and desist immediately.

"Hey, you," she called out.

No response.

As she drew closer, the toe of her boot unearthed a bull snake that slithered away in the dirt. Prairie dogs dove for their holes, while closer to her target several pups popped their heads up to see what was going on.

From fifty yards away, Angela could tell the person was a woman from the way she was dressed. She hadn't moved.

"Hey, I'm talking to you."

The woman remained still.

Drawing to within twenty feet, Angela knew why. The woman was positioned with her head on the ground, knees tucked beneath her, butt up in the air. Her arms were sprawled to her sides. Her face was turned sideways, with one eye opened in the blank stare of the dead.

Chapter 2

"Mom!"

Angela turned around and found Leroy Henderson two steps behind her.

Leroy bolted forward. Angela caught him around the waist. "Stop!"

"Let me go! That's my mom," he yelled.

Angela turned him away from the scene and held him tight. "You don't know that, Leroy. We have to go back."

Her heart broke for the young boy in her arms. Despite her words, she suspected he would recognize his own mother. She remembered how she felt when she had found her partner, Ian, dead. She had known immediately that it was him. Her next thought was to figure out who killed him.

Angela patted Leroy's back, wishing she were better with platitudes. Even as a child, she'd shied away from emotions. Two breakups and Ian's death had only reinforced her tendency to call things like she saw them. The best thing she could do for him was find out what had happened to his mother.

Crawford ran toward them through the field. "What is it?"

"You need to go back, Ms. Crawford. Get the kids on the bus. Now!" Angela ordered.

Crawford kept coming across the prairie dog mounds. "Is Leroy hurt? Leroy, are you okay? What happened? Did he get bitten by an animal? A prairie dog? Or a snake?"

"No," Angela said. "Stop and turn around."

"Let me go," Leroy screamed, kicking at Angela's shin. "That's my mom!"

Crawford frowned, and then looked past them toward the fence. Shock registered on her face. "Oh my lord, that's Sheila Henderson."

A positive ID. Angela wanted to ask the teacher when she'd last seen the victim, but didn't because of the boy in her arms.

"Take Leroy." she said. "Have the bus driver take you back to the Visitors Center. Wait for me there. Call everyone's parents. We'll send officers to get Leroy's father."

Crawford didn't move. She just stared at the victim.

"Crawford, did you hear me?" Angela used her free arm to turn the teacher around and push her back toward the road, all the while holding the sobbing boy.

"Yes, yes." Crawford pivoted, and then seemed to rally her senses. "Mr. Burton," she shouted. "Get the children back on the bus." Then she reached for Leroy. "Come with me, honey."

Leroy collapsed into his teacher's arms, and Angela breathed a sigh of relief. Now she could get down to business.

Turning, Angela walked the twenty feet back to the body. She reached down and felt for a pulse, then pulled out her cell phone. Canon picked up on the third ring. "Wayne, we have a situation in Section 5. I just found a body."

"You what?"

Angela filled him in. "I have no idea what happened. What's the protocol here?"

"Where are the kids?"

"Crawford's getting them back on the bus, and I'm sending them back to the Visitors Center. Apparently, it's the mother of one of the students." She told him about Leroy. She could hear Wayne rustling papers, and waited for him to give her direction.

"The first thing we have to do is notify the DOI that we have a serious incident. We're required to do that within fifteen minutes. Has it been that long?"

"Give or take."

"Document the exact time you found her. I'll make the call, and then head out to where you are. Meanwhile, notify the Adams County Sheriff's office and have them send out a team. We're going to treat this like a crime scene. With an unattended death, I'm sure the guys in Washington will want a full investigation."

"You'll need to bring out some crime scene tape," Angela said, watching the bus turn around and pull away. Everything she had was back in her truck at the Visitors Center. "What about a victim's advocate?"

"Hold off on that. I'll send Sharon over to the Visitors Center to get everyone's names and start the process of calling parents."

Sharon was Wayne's secretary, a pleasant woman who would be good with the kids. Angela was glad for that. "What about Leroy Henderson's father?"

"Have Adams County send someone over to pick him up."

"Roger that." Angela disconnected, then backtracked to the edge of the road and called Adams County dispatch to get officers on the way. After that, she pulled out her birding notebook and scribbled details of the scene. There wasn't much to note.

Time of discovery: approximately 8:55 a.m.

The victim: a woman.

Blond, roughly 5'7" and one hundred twenty-five pounds. Angela put the woman in her forties. From her position there didn't appear to be any visible signs of trauma, but Angela needed the coroner on scene to move the body. The surrounding area was disturbed, but that could have been caused by a number of things—the victim herself, Angela, or any number of animals.

The bigger question was: what was she doing out here? This was a restricted area—no visitors allowed. The perimeter fence to the east was at least a mile away. Had she come over the fence and then stumbled or crawled to where Angela had found her? More likely she'd been dumped right here.

Sirens in the distance signaled the sheriff department's arrival. A white patrol car followed by a cloud of dust snaked down 72nd. The vehicle slid to a stop beside Angela and a young deputy jumped out.

"What's the situation?" he asked, starting toward the prairie dog town.

"Hold up," Angela said. "The DOI wants this processed like a crime scene."

"DOI?"

"Department of the Interior. The OLES, Office of Law Enforcement and Security."

The deputy looked at Angela and narrowed his eyes. "Protocol requires we determine that she's dead."

Angela squinted at his name badge. She'd only been on the job two years, but this kid had to be fresh out of the academy. "Trust me, Deputy Tanner, I know dead. We need to wait for CSI before we go back out there."

Tanner puffed up his chest. "I think maybe I should check it out, just to be sure, before I call for a crime scene unit."

"If you go out there, you could destroy evidence," Angela said, stepping between the deputy and the field.

A modern Mexican standoff. Two sides versus three, yet a still untenable position. Fortunately for the deputy, the cavalry arrived in the form of Wayne Canon before things could escalate.

"Where are the CSIs?" Canon asked, jumping out of his truck. "OLES wants the scene processed."

Tanner stepped in front of Canon and held up his hand. "I'm the responding officer. I will be the one to make that determination."

"This is federal land," Wayne countered. "DOI is ultimately in charge. As part of Homeland Security, they're sending out someone from the F.B.I."

"For a body? Even before there's been an investigation?"

Wayne stared down the officer. "Until we know what this woman was doing on restricted government property, we will investigate all possibilities. The Army still maintains some destructive agents on site."

"What the hell is he talking about?" Tanner looked a little wild-eyed.

Angela waited to hear Wayne's response. There was no way she was going to jump into the conversation at this point. What she considered public knowledge might to him be "need to know."

Wayne cleared his throat. "The Army retains seven hundred twenty-five acres just north of here, with two landfills packed with toxic materials."

Tanner's eyes narrowed. "What type of materials?"

"Are you new around here?" Angela asked. Anyone who'd been

around here for more than a couple of years knew this was a Superfund site.

"Why?"

"This is the old Rocky Mountain Arsenal. They used to make chemical weapons here during World War II."

Tanner's mouth gaped open. "Are you telling me the Army is storing leftover bombs out here?"

"Not storing bombs. Not that anyone's aware of," Wayne said. "Now get on the phone and get the team headed this way."

Angela decided now was not the time to bring up the discovery of several forty to fifty-year-old Sarin gas bomblets in a scrap metal pile near the south-side perimeter fence in 2000. The Army had later admitted that there may still be additional materials scattered about the Refuge—a fact USFW and Commerce City wanted to keep quiet.

"If there's no danger, why is DOI involved?"

"They just need assurance that there hasn't been any breach," Wayne said. "Everything is kept in capped landfills and monitored according to EPA standards. It's just protocol."

Tanner jerked his head in the direction of a cluster of warehouse buildings to the west. "Is that Army headquarters?"

"The Army doesn't have an office on the Refuge," Angela said. "That's the National Eagle and Wildlife Property Repositories."

"What's stored there?" Tanner still sounded suspicious.

You need to do your homework. "That's where USFW keeps all the dead eagles, feathers and illegal wildlife trade products that are confiscated," she said.

"Are you talking stuff like ivory?"

"That and stuffed carcasses, jewelry, anything made from protected species. You name it, we've probably got it."

Tanner nodded. Angela figured he was trying to act knowledgeable on the subject, but the truth was, until you worked somewhere like the repository, you couldn't really understand the depth of the violations. Nothing seemed to be off limits. The National Wildlife Property Repository contained over 1.5 million items in all, everything from elephant tusks to leopard heads to crocodile skin purses. At the National

Eagle Repository over two thousand bald eagles were processed each year to fill more than six thousand applications for eagle parts. The repositories were founded in the 1970s, and the scary part was the trade in illegal wildlife had never slowed down.

While they waited for CSI to arrive, Wayne filled the time telling them stories of raids led by USFW on wildlife property traffickers in the state. Tanner listened with rapt attention, but looked relieved when the large white van lumbered up the road, being tailed by an unmarked car. He signaled them both toward the edge of the road.

"With any luck, maybe we'll be out of here before the feds show up," he said.

"Too late." Angela pointed first to herself and then to Wayne. "We're the feds."

Tanner ignored her and turned back to the CSI van. Four techs climbed out. The unmarked car pulled up and a man in a dark black suit climbed out. Angela's breath caught in her throat as he walked up and extended his hand to Wayne.

"Detective Sykes, Adams County Sheriff's office," he said, and then he turned and nodded at Angela. "Angel."

Wayne gave her a quizzical look.

"We go way back," she said by way of explanation, not really wanting to go into how they knew each other or why he was using her nickname. She'd met the handsome detective shortly after she'd been transferred to the repository. They'd kindled a romance. She'd fallen in love. He'd turned out to be a diehard bachelor. End of story.

Sykes gazed off across the field and then pointed to three of the techs. "You three, walk out to the body. Mark anything of interest. You," he instructed the fourth, "take pictures of everything."

"Be careful," Angela instructed. "Some of the mounds may have burrowing owls. They're protected."

"Leave it to me, Angel. My team knows what they're doing."

"Angela," she corrected. "And let's get something straight, Sykes. The body's on Ffederal land, which makes me lead on this case. Adam's County contributes professional services, but technically this is federal jurisdiction. You work for me. You got that?"

"Down, girl." He said, raising his hands in mock surrender.

Angela's anger spiked at his cavalier attitude. She started toward him, intending to get in his face, but Wayne headed her off.

"Sykes, you can run your team, but Angela's right. She's got final say on this." He shot her a warning glance. "Play nice." Dusting his hands together, he started toward his truck. "I'm heading back to the office. Call me if anything interesting turns up."

Twenty-five minutes later, Angela still fumed that Wayne had abandoned her here with Sykes. Not that he knew anything about their history. Admittedly, she had kept that to herself. But, he definitely noticed how Sykes's presence upset her. She could have used the backup.

Avoiding looking at Sykes, who was seated in his air-conditioned vehicle, Angela leaned against the fender of Tanner's patrol car and waited for CSI to issue the all-clear. When Rudy, the camera tech, finally signaled, she pushed off the fender of the patrol car and took out across the field. "We're up."

Tanner dogged her heels. "Hey, wait for me."

Angela heard the ding of a car door and felt a flash of satisfaction when she reached the body first. "What do you have?"

"Not much. There's no apparent sign of foul play. The vic has no ID," said Rudy.

Angela looked down at the corpse. "Her son and his teacher both identified her as Sheila Henderson."

Sykes had caught up by then and squatted beside the body to catch his breath. "Any idea what killed her?"

Rudy shook his head. "We just process the scene. I can't flip her over until the coroner shows."

That meant more standing around. The CSIs set up a shade tent to shield the body from the sun and now the seven of them waited. Sykes back in his car, the rest gathered around the CSI van and patrol car. Finally, the coroner and two assistants showed up, followed swiftly by two men in suits.

"Who are these guys?" Tanner asked.

"If I had to guess," Angela answered. "I'd say they're FBI."

"Sorry we're late." The coroner was a young woman, who—if

Angela's memory served—had recently been elected to the position. When Angela didn't ask her to elaborate, she walked over to the body and bent down. "Let's bag her. I'll know more when we can get her on the table in the lab."

"Not so fast!" one of the suits said, flipping open a badge. "FBI. Before you touch the body, we need a recap of what's gone on here."

Angela brought them up to speed. "I'll be coordinating the investigation. Let me give you my card."

With a pointed look at Sykes, she dealt her business cards out to the other principals and collected five back. She would need a scorecard to keep everyone straight.

"We'll need copies of any and all documentation," said one of the suits.

"Me, too," said Sykes.

"Me three," said Deputy Tanner.

Angela wished she could see everyone's eyes through their sunglasses. Tanner seemed to be looking between Sykes and her. She briefly considered putting on her own shades, when a yell from one of the coroner's assistants caused them all to turn.

"Snake!" The assistant pointed at a mound near the body.

Deputy Tanner charged forward. "What kind?"

"How the hell should I know? A rattlesnake. What other snake makes noise when you approach it?"

Tanner drew his weapon, but Angela blocked his shot.

"Put the gun away," she ordered. She turned to the assistant. "Did you get a look at it?"

"No. I moved away."

Angela looked around at the equipment. "Does anybody have a shovel?"

"In the van," said one of the CSIs.

"Do you mind getting it, please?"

While he lit out for the parked vehicles, Angela waited. If she was right, they wouldn't need it. But if it was a rattlesnake, a shovel would do the trick. First she'd try coaxing it back down into the burrow. If it decided to strike and hit the shovel blade, she would chop off its head.

The tech returned, handing over a short handled spade. Angela thanked him, then stepped around the body, getting as close as she could to the mound. Keeping the shovel between herself and the burrow, she moved the blade close to the entrance and heard the warning of the western diamondback.

Everyone took a step back—everyone that is but Angela, a couple of curious prairie dogs, and Rudy. He kept his camera pointed on the opening to the burrow.

Angela squatted to get a better look inside. The sun's direction made it hard to see. When she reached for the flashlight on her duty belt, her movement pressed the blade closer to the mound. Again, she heard the rattle.

"It's not backing down," Deputy Tanner said.

"It's not striking either." Angela flicked on her light. "I don't think we're dealing with a snake."

Rudy moved in closer behind her. "What else could it be?"

"Owls," Angela said. "Burrowing owls." She shined her light into the burrow. Six sets of yellow eyes gleamed in the darkness. "They mimic the rattlesnake buzz to deter predators."

"It worked." Rudy clicked off a few pictures. "What's all that crap around the opening?" He reached forward to pull something free.

"Don't touch that!" Angela ordered. "It's against federal law to disturb their nests."

"You're sure that's part of the nest?"

Angela nodded. "The owls line their burrows with dried cow dung and decorate the entrances with all sorts of objects—feathers, shredded paper, foil, and plastic."

"So, it really is crap."

Rudy snapped a few more pictures, and then the coroner's assistants moved back into position to remove the body. About that time, the two suits and Detective Sykes headed back across the field.

Angela felt both relieved and disappointed to see him go. She liked rubbing his nose in her authority, but it also annoyed her he hadn't bothered to tell her he was going. Maybe she wasn't totally over him after all? Then again, maybe—

"I think we're done here," the coroner said, interrupting her thoughts. "We have a pathologist on staff that does the autopsies in-house. I'll mark this one a priority."

"I appreciate that."

"It still may be a couple of days before I have any preliminary answers for you."

"Understood." Angela watched as the body was bagged and loaded into the wagon, then the coroner shook Angela's hand.

"Again, so you know, we just came from the scene of a homicide. There is definitely one ahead of you in the queue."

"How about the official report?" Angela asked. "How long before we can expect that?"

"Ten to twelve weeks," the coroner said. "If you're lucky."

Chapter 3

It hadn't taken long for Tanner to grow bored after the coroner and her assistants departed. Angela watched him fidget and waited for him to bail.

Finally, he jammed his hands in his pockets and looked toward the road. "I guess I'm not needed around here anymore, but I don't see your truck anywhere, Agent. Can I give you a lift somewhere?"

Angela glanced at the CSIs bagging evidence. "I probably need to stay out here."

"Nah, you can go if you want," Rudy volunteered. "We're going to be here a while."

Angela waffled. It had been a couple of hours since she had sent the two teachers and grade-schoolers back on the bus. It might be a good idea to check-in. "Are you sure you're okay without me?"

"We've got this."

"These animals need to be protected."

"Trust me, we'll steer clear of the owls," Rudy said. "The dung's a great deterrent."

His jokes made Angela more insecure about leaving them out there unsupervised. "How much longer are you planning to be?"

"My guess? A couple more hours."

"If I'm not back before you leave, call me." Angela said. "I'll be coming back out to make sure nothing has been disturbed."

"Don't worry. We'll be careful of your prairie dogs and the little family of owls."

"The parliament," Angela said. "They're called a parliament of owls."

Angela hitched a ride back to the Visitors Center with Tanner, and by the time they got there she was beginning to wish she had walked. In the ten minutes it took them to load up, turn around and drive to the center, she'd learned more about Tanner than she'd ever wanted to know. He was from the Midwest. He didn't like the grocery store layouts here. He was single, and struggled to make friends. She nearly cheered when he cut the vehicle's engine and she was free to get out.

"Thanks for the ride." She didn't wait for his response as she headed for the building, dreading what she might find waiting inside. But instead of a crowd, only Wayne's secretary, Sharon, the two teachers, and Leroy remained.

"All the other children were picked up by their parents," Sharon said, tipping her head in Leroy's direction. "He's the only one left. He asked us to leave him alone."

"What about his father?"

"Wayne dispatched two officers to pick him up at his work, but he'd already left. According to the girl who answered the phone, someone had called, told him there'd been an emergency and that he needed to pick up Leroy. I figure he's somewhere en route."

Angela glanced between the teachers and Leroy. "What about calling a victim's advocate?"

"I already did. But no one's shown up. Maybe just as well. Like I said, the boy asked to be left alone."

Angela thanked Sharon and walked over to where Leroy sat by himself in a chair behind the information desk. "How are you doing, kiddo?"

He looked up at her with stricken eyes. "They can't find my dad."

"I'm so sorry." she said, sliding onto the edge of the desk.

"You think he might have taken off? Your dad?" Deputy Tanner asked. "Do you think he'd have reason to hurt your mom, kid?"

No wonder the man didn't have friends. "Tanner!"

Leroy's eyes started to tear up. "My dad's a great guy."

Angela reached out and touched the boy's shoulder. "Ignore him. He's a butthead."

Leroy looked surprised. "Can you call him that?"

"If the shoe fits..." Angela glared at Tanner, daring him to say anything. "Is there something we can get you, Leroy? Do you feel like a soda?"

The kid shrugged.

"How about a root beer or 7-up? I'm sure Deputy Tanner would love to spring for one. It's the least he can do."

Tanner folded his arms across his chest. Angela figured he was trying to look cool. "You've got to stay hydrated, kid. What do you want?"

Leroy shrugged again. "A root beer, I guess."

As Tanner headed for the soda machine, Angela called out, "I'll take a Diet Coke."

This time, he glared at her over his shoulder.

Angela looked back at Leroy. "Sometimes these guys don't have a clue what they're doing."

Leroy gave her a straight-line grin.

"Seriously though, we do need to ask you a few questions."

Leroy looked down at his hands in his lap and nodded.

"When was the last time you saw your mom?"

"Last night."

"She didn't take you to school this morning?"

Leroy shook his head. "No. My dad did."

Angela made a note to check with Crawford.

"And earlier, you said your mom didn't like prairie dogs."

"She hated 'em."

Angela nodded. "So do you have any idea what she might have been doing out in the prairie dog town?"

Leroy answered in a virtual whisper. "I heard my dad tell her that if she planned to get rid of the prairie dogs near the soccer fields, she'd have to get proof they had bad fleas."

Angela considered the idea that Sheila was trying to collect samples, but she didn't remember seeing any collection vials.

"Do you know what happened to her?" Leroy whispered.

Angela felt her heart fracture. "No, I don't, Leroy. But we're going to find out. I promise."

"Here you go."

She jumped at the sound of Tanner's voice behind her. Accepting the Diet Coke he offered, she handed Leroy a root beer. As he popped the top on his soda, Crawford called out from the door of the staff office.

"Hold on," she said, starting toward them. "We don't allow the students to have sugary drinks."

Angela stood up, ready to do battle, when Burton moved into the doorway.

"Give the kid a break, Tammy," he said. "I think we can make an exception here."

Crawford gave a little shake of her head. "You know how it hypes him up."

Leroy started to take a sip of his drink, when a man pounded on the Visitors Center's door.

"Dad!"

Burton hurried over to let him in. "Mr. Henderson."

Angela took measure of the man entering the lobby. Tall, with a wild shank of light brown hair, he was dressed in blue jeans, work boots and a short-sleeved plaid shirt. His gaze darted around the room until it lit on Leroy.

"What are you accusing my son of doing this time?" he demanded, charging forward across the lobby. "And why are the police here? You can't question him about anything without Sheila or me present. Are you okay, son?"

Leroy's eyes brimmed with tears.

"What have they done to you?"

"Nothing," Angela said, stepping forward. "And Leroy hasn't done anything wrong."

"Then what the hell is going on? I just got called off a project. My secretary said there was some kind of an emergency."

"Mr. Henderson, would you please sit down?" Angela pointed to a chair near the information desk. "We need to talk to you."

"No, I won't sit down. I want to know what this is about." Henderson was clearly agitated. Tanner's hand edged toward his gun.

"It's about your wife, Mr. Henderson," Angela said.

Crawford stepped forward "We're so sorry."

"Sorry? About what?" Henderson scanned the faces, and then turned back to Angela. He seemed to have lost some of his energy. "What's going on here? Where's Sheila?" He looked at his son. "Leroy?"

The boy started crying and Angela rested her hand on his shoulder. "Mr. Henderson, I'm sorry to be the one to inform you, but your wife is dead."

Chapter 4

Either Ron Henderson was one heck of an actor or he didn't know anything about what had happened to his wife. It had taken them the better part of an hour to calm him down enough to ask him a few more questions. All he'd been able to verify was that Sheila had said she had an early morning meeting and had asked him to get Leroy up and drop him at school. The last time he had seen Sheila was around 5:00 a.m.

It was late afternoon by the time Angela had gotten back to her desk at the repository. After filling out the paperwork required by the DOI and faxing it to Washington, she input all of the phone numbers and email addresses she'd collected into her cell phone and filed the business cards.

Wayne strode into her office as she was putting the last one away. "So where do we stand on this?"

Angela gave him a recap.

"You know, we need to stay on top of things. OLES isn't going to let this go until we have some answers."

Angela's head hurt. Lacing her fingers through her hair, she closed her eyes and rubbed her temples with the palm of her hands. "There's nothing more we can do, Wayne. We won't know what happened until we get the coroner's preliminary report."

"Any idea why she was in the prairie dog town?"

"Her son suggested she was there to collect fleas. She wanted to try and prove that the prairie dogs carry the plague."

"You're telling me that she left her house early, drove onto the Refuge to cause trouble for us, and got herself murdered causing trouble for us?"

Angela sighed. "For all we know, she died of natural causes. Until we get the autopsy report, it's all speculation."

"I want to know the minute that report comes in."

His tone carried an urgency that made Angela open her eyes and stare at him. Wayne started jabbing his finger into the air. "Every single one of the entities that were out there today—the sheriff's department, the coroner's office and the FBI—will be conducting their own investigation. We need to find out what the CSI team uncovers and solve this case, before any of the others do."

Angela lowered her hands to her desk. "Why?"

"What do you mean, why?"

"Why do we have to beat everyone else? What matters is finding her killer."

"Sure, but it happened on our watch. The DOI is going to be watching how we handle this case."

"It's not like it was our fault, Wayne."

"Easy to say, but you know how bureaucracies are. We don't need any challenge to our jurisdiction nor anyone questioning our ability to solve the crime. You need to assert yourself as lead agent. Speaking of that," he said, moving closer to her desk. "What's the deal with you and Detective Sykes? Why do I sense there's some bad blood between you?"

Angela looked down at her hands. "It's personal, Wayne."

"Personal like you've had a previous run-in, or personal like you know each other outside of the job?"

"Personal like it's none of your business."

"So...outside the job."

Angela looked up to find him studying her. "I can handle him."

Wayne stabbed his finger at her. "Don't let it interfere with the investigation. I'd take it on, but I'm in the middle of budgets."

That explained why he seemed so stressed. "So, that's what this turf war is about? Budgets? Are you afraid if we don't solve this case Washington might cut your funding?"

"Let's just say, for the sake of job security, it would behoove you to make sure that the powers that be appreciate the need for law enforcement out here." He moved back toward the door. "I expect you to get me some answers. Capiche?"

Angela thought about how much she enjoyed her job and reached for her keys. "I'm all over it."

Following him out, she locked up and then headed for home. After eating some packaged macaroni and cheese, she took a shower and tumbled into bed, but sleep eluded her. She tossed and turned, and couldn't stop thinking about Sykes. It annoyed her how quickly he'd grown bored with the investigation into Sheila Henderson's death. But then, finding answers for the family or justice for the victim was never top on his list. His interest always lay more with nailing the perpetrator and collecting the accolades that came with being a hotshot detective. That and lording it over his friends and colleagues. She knew considering their history that working with him was going to be difficult. She also knew it fell into her camp to try and broker a peace.

In the early hours of the morning, Angela gave up on sleep. Sitting outside on her balcony, she watched the sunrise. Then, grabbing a cup of coffee, she headed for work, detouring past the sheriff's office looking for Sykes. She found him hunkered over his desk.

"Hey," she said.

"Angel."

His use of the nickname caused her blood pressure to spike. It was reserved for people like her father and close friends, people who loved and cared about her. Then, reminding herself she was there to broker a peace, she drew a breath and started over. "I stopped by to fill you in on where things stand with the case."

He looked up and grinned. "I don't really have time for this now. I've been assigned lead on last night's homicide."

His swift dismissal caught her off guard. "That's great news for you, but I thought you were the Arapaho County Liaison on the Henderson case."

"Not anymore."

"What's the deal with the homicide? Any chance it's connected to my case? I mean, two suspicious deaths in one day, and both in Commerce City. Don't you think that's an odd coincidence?" Arapahoe County saw its share of violent crime, about 39 murders a year and Commerce City claimed half of the total. But with only 16 homicides a year, having two on the same day was rare.

"Nah, it's just one of those weird things. I can't see how they're related. Besides, there's no official ruling that your victim didn't die of natural causes." Sykes clicked off his computer and started to gather his things. "Look, until they say it's a homicide, it's not of interest to major crimes."

That raised Angela's hackles. "Well someone in the Arapahoe Sheriff's Office has to liaise, Sykes. The USFW has an agreement whereby you handle the forensic work."

"Then I suggest you check with Tanner. He was the first officer on the scene. Plus, he seems to have developed a bit of a crush on you."

Kiss my tush, Sykes. She considered a few other choice remarks, then settled for, "Thanks, I'll track him down."

Tanner was nowhere to be found. After checking with the desk sergeant and leaving the rookie a message, Angela headed over to the coroner's office, hoping she might have some preliminary results on the autopsy. The receptionist there sent Angela down to the morgue.

The autopsy room took up most of the basement. The walls were painted white and floor was covered in white tiles. Stainless steel sinks lined one wall. Body lockers lined another. An antiseptic smell complemented the look.

The staff pathologist stood in the middle of the room. He'd just loaded Sheila Henderson's body onto the slab. "I'm just getting started, but you're welcome to stay."

Angela forced a smile. Autopsies weren't high on her to-do list.

"Thanks," she said, "but maybe I should just leave you to it. What I'm after is the probable cause of death."

"If I were to hazard a guess, I'd say she died from an epidural hematoma. A blow to the head. To be exact, a blow to her temple." The pathologist signaled for Angela to move closer. "Do you see here? This was the side of her head facing the ground." He pulled her hair apart and showed Angela the scalp near the temple. "Can you see the marks? Once I shave her head I think we'll find bruising, which may give us an idea of the murder weapon. My guess is we'll find massive hemorrhaging on the inside of her skull. Look at her eye. See how the pupil on the right is enlarged? And there's clear fluid draining from her ear.

"So you're saying someone hit her?"

The pathologist dropped the clump of the victim's hair. "I'm saying she suffered a blow to the head. It's possible someone hit her. It's also possible she had an accident, maybe suffered a fall and hit her head."

"Except there is no sign of her car and she was half a mile or more away from the nearest fence," Angela said.

"Could she have jumped the fence? It's possible she hit her head on a rock." The coroner reached toward a small tray lined with instruments and Angela stepped back.

"The burrow where we found her is over a mile from the Refuge perimeter. How could she could have walked that far after suffering a severe blow to the head?"

"It is possible. These types of head injuries are unpredictable. She may have lost consciousness briefly, come around and even resumed her scheduled activities until experiencing a sudden onset of symptoms."

"Seriously? How long could she have been fine?"

The pathologist shrugged and reached for a scalpel. "It's hard to say. A person might seem okay for as many as six to eight hours, and then suddenly die. Other times, a person will start showing symptoms within minutes or fall immediately into a coma and never regain consciousness."

The pathologist pressed the scalpel to the body and Angela took a step toward the door.

"So, from what you're saying, the victim could have sustained this head injury as early as midnight the morning she was found."

"It's possible." The pathologist relaxed his arm. "Do you remember Natasha Richardson?"

"The actress?"

"Right. Now she suffered a head injury while skiing and checked out fine. It wasn't until an hour or so later that she started showing symptoms—a headache, blurred vision, slurred speech. We call it 'talk and die'-syndrome. But I won't know for sure that's what happened here until I get inside this woman's brain."

"Any idea how long her body had been out in that field?"

"Temperatures cool down at night, but there were no signs of any predation. I think we could expect that if she'd been out there very long. Best guess, a couple of hours."

As the pathologist made the first cut to Sheila Henderson's chest, Angela backed out the door. The new time frame meant one of two things had happened. First case scenario, sometime between midnight and 8:30 a.m., Henderson hit her head on something. Then, in the morning, she drove out to the Refuge and died. That would make her death an accident. Second case scenario, sometime between those hours, someone conked Shelia Henderson on the head. In that case, it didn't matter how long she lived after the fatal blow. It would still be murder.

After reaching the parking lot, Angela sat in her truck, rolled down the windows to allow in the cool morning air and considered her next move. If Sheila was murdered, the next order of business was to learn more about her and establish a timeline of her last twenty-four hours. That meant talking to people who knew her. Sheila's husband, Ron, had made it clear that his wife was a stay-at-home mom. He'd claimed she'd left home around 5:30 a.m. the morning she died. Also according to him, she was the de facto leader of the soccer moms. He'd given Angela a few names. At the top of the list was Patricia Litchfield, Sheila's best friend and confidant. It seemed like as good a place as any to start.

Chapter 5

The Litchfield's lived two houses down from the Henderson's, in an upper middle-class neighborhood on the north side of the Refuge, in one of the newer housing developments. Large, multi-level houses in shades of tan and blue were packed in tightly side-by-side on wide streets that curved through the development. Each house had a two-car garage, and a square of grass with trees planted near the sidewalks and fenced backyards. She guessed the median income of the residents in this development was encroaching on six figures.

Passing the Henderson's house, Angela took note of the drawn shades and the paper still on the front stoop. She pictured the father and son inside, sitting and staring at the walls, both paralyzed with grief. Based on her observations of the day before, she couldn't imagine how the two of them were going to survive.

Parking on the street in front of the Litchfield's home, Angela walked up the driveway, onto the front walk, then climbed the steps to the porch and knocked. The door was answered by a woman wearing a terrycloth bathrobe. Her dark hair was clipped up in a rat's nest of curls. Puffy, red eyes showed she'd been crying.

"Patricia Litchfield?"

"Yes?"

"I'm Agent Angela Dimato with U.S. Fish and Wildlife. I'm investigating Sheila Henderson's death. Do you mind if I ask you a few questions?"

"This is really not a good time," Litchfield said.

It was never a good time. "I understand," Angela said. "It won't take long. It's important."

Litchfield hesitated, then stepped back from the door and headed into the bowels of the house. "Close the door behind you, please."

Angela shut the door and followed the woman past a large open living room area and a dining room, into a bright, airy kitchen. A breakfast nook looked out into a postage stamp-sized back yard, surrounded by a six-foot high security fence.

"Would you like a cup of coffee?" Litchfield said, waving toward a seat at the table.

Angela pulled out a chair. "Only if it's already made."

A few minutes later, Litchfield joined her at the table carrying two steaming mugs of coffee and a plate with two blueberry muffins. "So what do you want to know?"

"I realize this is hard, Mrs. Litchfield."

"Patty. I go by Patty." She pushed a muffin in Angela's direction.

Angela took it and peeled back the wrapping. "I'm trying to figure out why Sheila Henderson was inside the Refuge, crawling around near a burrow of owls."

"She wouldn't have hurt them, if that's what you think. She loved birds."

Angela picked at a blueberry and sipped her coffee. "Maybe, but her son told me that she didn't much like the prairie dogs."

"Who does?" Patty Litchfield set her mug down hard, sloshing coffee over the sides. "They're nasty little creatures that leave holes all over the soccer fields. And of all people, you must know that the dirty little rodents carry bubonic plague. Four Adam's County residents have died this year."

Angela was aware of the deaths and none of them were connected to the prairie dogs on or near the Refuge. In all four cases, the victims had come in contact with plague-positive fleas carried on rats living in their homes.

"Do you think Sheila was in the Refuge trying to collect evidence of the disease?"

"I suppose it's possible, but that doesn't really sound like Sheila. All she wanted was for the city to put up a special barrier, to contain the prairie dogs and keep them off the school grounds."

"What kind of barrier?"

"Some type of visual barrier." Patty pushed her hair back. "Sheila read about it in some engineering magazine of Ron's. The article claimed that if you hung some sort of blackout tarping low on a fence, it would block the prairie dogs' ability to see beyond it and make them hesitant to cross the barrier. It's expensive, but completely humane. Sheila was against the normal types of control, like shooting or poisoning the animals. She said that killed the birds and, like I said, she liked birds."

Angela watched tears well up and then spill from Patty's eyes. The woman reached for a tissue.

"So Sheila appealed to the city to fund this fence?" Angela said, taking another bite of her muffin. She noticed Patty hadn't touched hers.

"That's right. She originally petitioned the school, but the school board wouldn't consider it. It was after that she approached the city council for money. They refused, too, but she was prepared. She filed a lawsuit against the school district, and she would have won. She knew her way around the system."

"How so?"

Patty dabbed at her tears. "Before Sheila and Ron got married, she was a legal secretary. That woman was never afraid to fight for what she believed in. She decided if the school board and city council didn't want to build us a fence, she would force the issue."

"By doing what?"

"She filed a lawsuit over the conditions of the soccer field. We have kids from kindergarten to high school that play ball on the field, and several kids have been hurt running into a prairie dog mound. It's only a matter of time before someone catches the plague."

"Did she file this suit on behalf of the soccer league?"

Patty shook her head. "The soccer league didn't want anything to do with it, but most of the soccer moms are behind her. It's our kids that are getting hurt out there."

"So she filed on behalf of herself?"

"No, she filed on Leroy's behalf. Last year he stepped in a hole and broke his ankle. Sheila filed a one million dollar lawsuit against the school district for medical bills, pain, and suffering."

"What happened?" Angela asked.

Patty leaned forward. "The school suspended the soccer program for the upcoming year pending the outcome. It made some of the parents mad. One father in particular. He threatened her. He said she'd be sorry if she didn't drop the lawsuit."

Angela could see how shutting down a major recreational program would have the potential to make people angry. Setting aside the rest of her muffin, she dug her notebook out of her pocket. "What was the man's name?"

Patty sat back. "Oh, he didn't really mean it. He was just mad, you know?"

"I'd still like to talk to him." Angela found a pen and looked up at Patty. The woman looked away, twisting the tissue in her hand.

"You have to understand," Patty said. "His son is a senior this year. The family was counting on a soccer scholarship for him to go to college. He would have been the first one in his family. I've never seen Ron so mad."

"Sheila's husband?

Patty nodded.

"You can't really blame him," Angela said. "The soccer dad threatened his wife."

"Oh, Ron wasn't mad at Ken. He was furious with Sheila. He claimed it made Leroy a target for bullies, as if anything or anyone could scare that kid." Patty shook her head. "Of course, they'd been having some problems."

"Ron and Sheila?" Angela asked. That was a new twist.

Patty nodded. "Sheila told me she thought Ron was having an affair."

"With who?"

Patty suddenly stood and shoved back her chair.

"I think I've said too much." Patty picked up her mug and the plate and walked over to the kitchen sink. "I think I'd like you to leave now."

That was her cue. Angela stood and carried her own mug to the sink. "Look, your friend is dead. I know you want to help me find out what happened to her. I really need those names."

Patty looked up from the sink. Angela tried to smile encouragingly. She could see the doubt flicker through the woman's eyes.

"Ken Martinez," she finally said. "That's the name of the man who threatened Sheila."

"And the woman she thought was having an affair with her husband?"

Patty looked back at the sink and started rinsing the mugs. Angela waited. When she finally spoke, her voice was barely a whisper.

"Ellie. Ellie Parker."

"Thank you." Angela considered reaching out and touching Patty's back, but then thought better of it. Comfort wasn't her strong suit. Even as a kid she'd never been much of a cuddler. The more professional she kept things, the better. "I can let myself out. Thanks for the coffee."

Patty's head dipped.

Angela was halfway to the door when she thought of one last question and turned around. "You said Sheila loved birds."

"So?" Patty said, stepping into the kitchen doorway.

"Did she ever go birding on the Refuge?"

"She went there all the time." Patty snickered. "That used to make Ron mad, too. Her favorite place to go was First Creek, over by the eagle's roost."

"Do you know what time she liked to go out?"

"Early in the morning, maybe 5:30 or 6:00 a.m."

That corroborated her husband's story. First Creek was off-limits to self-guided visitors. "I take it she drove over there."

"Of course, it's too far to walk." Patty stuffed her hands in the pockets of her robe and wrapped it tightly around her. "Sheila took me there once to see the bald eagles."

Angela made another mental note—to look near the roost for Sheila Henderson's car. After taking Leroy home yesterday afternoon, Ron had reported it missing. Tanner had issued an all-points-bulletin, but the car still hadn't been found. If it was on the Refuge, it wasn't in any of the obvious places—not in the Visitors Center parking lot or anywhere near where her body was found. It was a half-mile hike from the eagle's roost to the prairie dog town. A doable walk, especially if she wanted to hide her vehicle for some reason. Though what that reason could be, Angela had yet to fathom.

Chapter 6

It took ten minutes for Angela to get to the National Eagle Repository from Patty Litchfield's house, and there was a phone message from the coroner's office waiting. The pathologist had called confirming his suspicions. His findings showed that Sheila Henderson had indeed died from a blow to the head, causing massive internal bleeding in the brain. He concluded that, based on the bruising pattern, it appeared she'd been struck with some type of round, decorated object. The only other oddity was a sticky residue on her hands that they hadn't been able to identify.

"Anything new?" Wayne asked, popping his head through the doorway.

Angela clicked off the speaker phone and looked up. "The coroner's office has officially ruled that Sheila Henderson died of blunt force trauma. They've marked it a possible suspicious death. How or when she suffered the blow to the head is anyone's guess."

"We'll have to inform the OLES."

"Of course you will." Angela tried not to sound too sarcastic over his use of "we." "I also had a talk with the best friend." She told him about her conversation with Patty Litchfield. "She's positive Sheila would have had her car with her."

"Then where is it?"

That's the $64,000 question. "I don't know. Your guess is as good as mine. Maybe we should take a ride out to First Creek and take a look around."

Wayne nodded. "Why not? Give me fifteen minutes. I'll file the report with DOI, and meet you out front."

Once he had disappeared, Angela noted the time, then sat down at her desk and booted up her computer. She had three known people of interest—Ron Henderson, Ken Martinez, and Ellie Parker—and then there was Sykes's homicide to consider. Again she wondered about the coincidence of two deaths in one day in Commerce City, and made a mental note to push for more details.

Accessing the law enforcement database, she focused on the names she had. Of the three, Ken Martinez was the only one with a record. Ten years ago, he'd spent one night in jail for an assault at a local bar. All charges had been dropped the next day.

A Google search proved more fruitful.

Ron Henderson had a Linked-In page. His resume listed him as a civil engineer for the Colorado Department of Transportation. He had taken a job with CDOT straight out of college, started as an engineer-in-training in District 2, and moved up the ranks. He was now the Resident Engineer of District 1, overseeing road and bridge operations.

Ken Martinez didn't have a Linked-In page, but based on random articles in the Commerce City Sentinel, it appeared his biggest claim to fame was being the father of soccer superstar, Ken Jr. One write up listed his profession as shift supervisor at the local Walmart. He also had a daughter, who was a junior at Adam's City High School.

A Department of Motor Vehicle search turned up an Elizabeth Parker living in Commerce City. Angela searched the property database and found she co-owned a residence with Samuel Bernal Parker in the Reunion area north of the Refuge.

Her time up, Angela shut down the computer and hurried outside to find Wayne waiting impatiently beside his USFW truck. "I thought I was going to have to come up and get you. Get in."

Climbing up into the passenger seat, she rolled down the window and enjoyed the breeze as he headed out on 72nd, and pulled onto the Caps and Covers Road. It was a beautiful day. In the distance she could see the Denver skyline rising against the backdrop of the Continental Divide. A hawk spun lazy circles in the sky overhead and a small herd of white-tailed deer frolicked in the trees along the edge of Lower Derby Lake. When they reached Chambers Road, Wayne turned south. A chain with a "Closed to the Public" sign hung across the road, and Angela climbed out to open the gate. From there, the service road was just a track, two gravel strips with grass growing in the center—rutted and washed out from last year's floods. She kept her eyes open for any sign of a vehicle parked off the road.

"I don't see how Henderson could have got in here without someone seeing her," Wayne said, wrestling with the steering wheel of the truck. "What kind of car does she drive?"

"A 4Runner. Gray."

Just before the narrow bridge that marked the north end of the eagle's roost, Wayne pulled off into a small turnaround area. He parked the truck on the shortgrass under a large cottonwood tree. Angela climbed out and studied the tracks in the turnaround.

"I don't see any useable tire marks or footprints, but its clear several people have been out here recently."

"Don't disturb anything," Wayne said. "DOI will want CSI to confirm."

Angela bristled. She knew the protocol. Nothing like having your boss point out the obvious.

"We don't even know for sure that she was the one who was out here," she said.

"Who else could it have been?" Wayne fumbled in his pocket for his phone. "She's the only one dead, with a missing car, whose BFF said she loves birds."

While he called dispatch, Angela circled the area. On the west side of the clearing, she made a gruesome discovery—an eagle feather with a bloody quill.

Wayne punched off his phone. "Adam's County is sending a unit, along with Deputy Tanner." He jerked his head in her direction. "What do you have there?"

"A feather." Angela held it up. "It looks like it's been plucked from a bird."

"So maybe she wasn't collecting," Wayne said. "Maybe she was taking."

Angela nodded. "An actionable offense—if it was her. For all we know, it could have been anyone."

Animal-related crimes were what had compelled her to become an agent, and it sickened her whenever someone intentionally harmed wildlife to feather their own nest. She thrived on bringing the law to bear against them. And harvesting feathers from a Bald Eagle was not only illegal, it was reprehensible.

The Bald Eagle Protection Act of 1940 clearly stated it was against the law for anyone to possess or take, buy or sell, anything related to a bald eagle, dead or alive. That included all body parts, nests and eggs. The Act was amended in 1972 to include golden eagles, but the basics were clear—you couldn't so much as pick up a feather without facing charges.

A first violation could result in a $5,000 fine and imprisonment for one year. A second offense doubled the penalty. And there were stiffer penalties under the Migratory Bird Treaty Act. Noting the blood and skin around the base of the quill, this feather was recently pulled from the body of a bird. Whoever had done this deserved to have the book thrown at them.

Angela squatted down and studied the ground. "It looks like it happened recently."

"So let's say Sheila Henderson came down here looking for feathers and got caught," Wayne said.

Angela straightened up. "Then why clock her in the head and leave the feather behind? If they knew the value of the feather, why not take the feather? Or, better yet, turn her in for the reward?" According to the Act, anyone with information leading to a conviction received half of the fine assessed. Using Wayne's logic, if someone had caught her with an eagle feather, Sheila would have been the one with the motive for murder.

"I see your point." Wayne rubbed his hand across his mouth and scrunched up his face in thought. "Maybe she caught someone else in the act?"

That actually made more sense to Angela, but then where was the rest of the bird? Plucking feathers out of a cold carcass was hard work, and no one was going to yank a feather out of a live bird.

"And where the heck is her car?" Angela mused out loud. Finding it might fill in more of the gaps. "She had to get out here somehow."

"That's what I'm paying you to find out," Wayne said, heading back toward his truck. "I'm going back out to the road to wait for the deputy and CSI. Are you coming?"

"No, I'll keep looking around here," she said. Not that it mattered. Wayne was already gone.

Angela preferred being out here alone—listening to the breeze move through the trees and the call of a hawk, observing the lay of the land. Grounding herself in the setting was something Ian had taught her to do. By knowing what to expect, the incongruities in one's setting were easier to spot.

Once centered, she canvased a wider area and turned up a spot on the edge of the turnaround where a scuffle had taken place. There was more than the usual number of broken branches. Though she had to admit, it was possible the disturbance had been caused by the deer.

Heading back to the bridge, she crossed First Creek and retraced her steps along the west bank toward the eyrie. Finding no more signs of people, she stopped after a few hundred feet and took in the beauty. On the opposite side of the creek was a line of large cottonwoods, where, in January and February, the bald eagles shared a communal roost high in the trees. Currently, one tree at the most southerly end housed a nesting pair and their two fledglings. It was too far to see from where she stood, but Angela searched for a sign of the pair in the air. She saw none, hoping nothing bad had happened to either of them.

A loud whistle signaled Wayne's return and she turned back. In the minutes it took her to reach the turnaround, the techs were building molds to make casts of the tire impressions.

"I want to take a walk out to the nest, Wayne," Angela said. "The feather I found wasn't molted, which means someone pulled it off a bird. I want to make sure the nesting pair is okay."

He looked less than ecstatic, but said, "Why not?"

Leaving Tanner to supervise the tire casts, Wayne and Angela grabbed their binoculars, and hiked back along the road to the bridge. Crossing over the creek, they cut straight east into the open fields on a beeline trajectory to the spot where Sheila Henderson's body was found. Halfway to the crime scene tape, they cut south toward the nesting tree.

Angela walked slowly, keeping her eyes peeled for signs of disturbance. Shuffling marks on the ground gave clear indications that they weren't the only recent visitors. Angela used her phone and snapped a couple of photos.

"None of these will be of any use," Wayne said.

Always the curmudgeon. Though, to be fair, she had already come to the same conclusion.

"I just hope we don't find that the nest has been disturbed," she said, wishing she could silence the voice in her head telling her differently. It was something that began after Ian died. First she heard him in her head issuing warnings. Now it was just an inner voice, but time and experience had taught her to listen.

Selling eagle parts was lucrative. Wing feathers sold for as much as $150 a piece and tail feathers for $250. An eagle had twelve tail feathers, twenty primary wing feathers, and twenty-eight secondary wing feathers. Add in the other items of value, like the talons and beak, a full bird could net a seller upwards of $10,000.

Buyers were also easy to come by. The black market demand was huge. Private collectors paid thousands for Native American memorabilia, and there were growing numbers of non-Indians embracing Native American culture. Even among Native Americans, the demand had increased—with the wait-time as long as two-to-five years for legally obtained eagle parts.

Reaching the stand with the eyrie, Angela backed up deep into the field and trained her binoculars on the top of the tree. The nest still rested in the upper branches. Six or seven feet across and two feet deep, it appeared to be intact—a jumbled mass of sticks and twigs.

A shadow crossed the nest and Angela looked skyward. An adult bald eagle swept in, a large northern pike dangling from its talons. As if on cue, the two eaglets appeared, jumping up on the edge of the nest and screaming for food.

The adult eagle flew past and circled back, staying just out of reach, as if daring its youngsters to fly.

The eaglets strutted back and forth, their mouths open, demanding to be fed. Mostly brown, their wings and bodies were mottled with varying shades of white. At this stage, both of the parents spent most of their time hunting for food and the eaglets spent most of their time alone in the nest.

Angela let herself relax. So far, everything appeared to be fine. Looping her binoculars around her neck, she signaled to Wayne.

"What?" he said.

"Since we're out here, let's check out the crime scene. Maybe we missed something."

Together they moved toward the ring of yellow tape flapping at the edge of the prairie dog town. The wind blew errant strands of hair from her ponytail around her head, and Angela turned her face into the steady breeze. The sun beat down. With nothing else to go on, they needed to find Sheila Henderson's car. With any luck, they'd missed a clue, something that would point them in the right direction.

Chapter 7

The yellow and black tape encircled a large section of the prairie dog town, stretching one-thousand feet from the location of the body in every direction. The two-track path still referred to as E. 72nd Ave. served as the northern perimeter. Half a mile east, it intersected with a service road running parallel to Buckley Rd. To the south and west there were prairie dogs as far as the eye could see. It made her think of a song from the musical Oklahoma. She hated to admit it, but maybe you could have too much of a good thing.

"Let's check the fence." Angela struck out east along the road. She didn't really believe Sheila Henderson had crossed that way, but they needed to rule it out.

At the gravel service road, they turned south and walked along the ten foot chicken-wire fence that separated Buckley from the Refuge. On the outside of the barrier were places where people had pulled in and parked. Based on the scattered beer cans and cigarette butts, Angela figured high school kids out on a Saturday night. There were no signs that anyone had been on the ground inside the fence.

After walking about a thousand feet, Wayne turned around. "I say we head back."

"We've come this far," Angela said. "Let's go to the eagle watch."

If body language could be audible, then Wayne groaned. "Why?"

"Henderson's best friend Patty said Sheila liked to go there. Maybe she saw something out there, something that got her killed."

"Or maybe she died from heat stroke. I say we go back and get my truck, with its air conditioning."

"Whimp." Angela kept moving south, figuring Wayne would follow.

"Let's at least save ourselves some time," he said, heading out across the field. Prairie dogs scattered in all directions, some diving for their holes, some rising up on their haunches and barking from a safe distance.

"What are you doing?" Angela asked. The policy was to avoid walking through the prairie dog towns in the summer when the burrowing owls were nesting. "I ought to write you a ticket."

"Don't even think about it. I'm cutting a half-mile off our hike."

Angela hesitated, and then followed him. There were no burrowing owls in the heart of the prairie dog town. The worst thing that could happen is she or Wayne might cave in a mound or twist an ankle or run into a snake.

Reaching the eagle watch without incident, they stood on the wooden platform and scanned the area with their binoculars. Angela could see indications that someone had been out there in the past few days. But who? Sheila?

"It's possible she saw someone out near the eyrie from here," Angela said. "According to her best friend, she was very protective of the eagles. It likely would have set her off and forced a confrontation."

"She doesn't seem like the type who would have confronted someone alone. She seemed more the type to slap them with a lawsuit."

Touché. Angela would have been confrontational, but then, she did carry a gun. "What if Sheila had gotten in her car and headed for the repository to find a ranger?"

"Or maybe she just drove away." Wayne dropped his binoculars on his chest.

"Let's say she saw something," Angela said. "There are only two ways out—north or south."

Most visitors would have headed south to E. 64th St. and gone toward the Visitors Center. Technically the route was closed to sightseers past the Wildlife Drive turn-around, but the road was maintained. Rangers were constantly chasing people out of the restricted areas. The northern route followed the two-track road they had just walked in on, and was off limits to all visitors east of C St. Going that way, Sheila would have been on unmaintained roads until she reached the repositories. It wasn't the logical route to take, but if she was familiar with Rocky Mountain Arsenal property—and according to Patty Litchfield, she was—Sheila could have left in a hurry.

"Maybe someone spotted her and followed her?" Angela suggested.

"No, if she crashed her car on 64th, someone should have spotted it by now."

"Maybe, maybe not. There are several places heading toward the repository where a car might go off the road and remain hidden for months. Besides, there aren't very many of us who come out this far on a regular basis."

Cutting back through the fields, Angela kept her eyes open for signs that anyone had been out here walking besides them. But, except for the damage Wayne caused scuffling his feet on the dry ground, there was no sign of any human incursion. At Chambers, Wayne turned left.

"It's hot. I'm tired. I'm going to go get the truck."

Angela nodded, but pressed on, walking another four hundred feet before reaching a spot where the willows, skunkbrush, and cottonwoods pressed in tight along the road. From track marks, it looked like someone might have turned around. Sheila, or someone following her?

Before Angela could investigate further, Wayne pulled up in the truck. He rolled down the window, blasting her with country music and cold air. "Find anything?"

"Not yet." But the little voice in her head shouted for her to keep looking.

"Get in. We've wasted enough time out here. Tanner and the CSI are gone, and I've got things to do in the office."

She paced the edge of the road, and was about to give in when a flash of gray caught her eye. She squinted and stepped toward the embankment.

"Did you hear me?" Wayne said, inching the truck forward.

Angela ignored him and scrambled down the embankment. Pushing aside the branches, she found what they'd been looking for. Buried deep in the skunkbrush and perched on a patch of poison ivy sat Sheila Henderson's car.

"What the hell are you doing?" Wayne yelled. Angela heard the slam of a door.

"I found it, Wayne." Excitement spurred her forward through the bushes. There had to be a clue here, something that would help them figure out what happened.

"Is there any damage to the car?"

"Scratches." Angela forced aside more branches and discovered that the Jeep had plowed into a large cottonwood. The front end was crumpled, and the passenger side door was opened. "She hit a tree."

"That would explain the blow to the head," Wayne sounded happy to draw that conclusion. "Leave it! I'll call for a tow."

Angela peered inside the car, looking for something round and patterned that Sheila might have struck her head on. There was nothing. The gearshift was smooth and low on the console. She would have had to have been a contortionist to hit her head on the handle. Besides, based on the coroner's report, whatever she'd been struck by had left unusual markings on her scalp. From Angela's perspective, there was no possible way Sheila had died from hitting her head during the crash. Sheila Henderson had been murdered.

"Did you hear me?" hollered Wayne.

Angela backed away. The last thing she wanted to do was compromise the evidence. If there was a clue, CSI would find it. The key piece to the puzzle could come from anywhere—the dirt on the mats, fingerprints on the door handles, fibers on the seats. As much as she wanted to continue poking around, processing the car offered the best chance of finding evidence that would point them to the killer.

It took two hours for the car to be towed, and a preliminary examination of the vehicle didn't turn up anything. There was nothing tying Sheila Henderson to the eagle feather or to the eagle's nest overlook, and nothing tying the feather to the car. There was dirt from the turnaround on the driver's side floor mat, but no indication that more than one person had been in the car. The only good news was—despite all of Wayne's hoping—the coroner had stood behind his conviction that Sheila had died from a blow to the head by a foreign object. The steering wheel wasn't a match.

Now she was sure Sheila's death was a murder committed within an eight hour window, Angela decided it was time to pinpoint exactly where the woman had been between the hours of midnight and 8:00

a.m. on the morning of her murder. Her first stop was the Henderson's house off of E. 96th Street.

The shades were still drawn when she pulled up in front, and another paper had been added to the stoop. It didn't look like anyone had been in or out in the past two days. Stepping over the papers, Angela knocked on the front door. It opened to the length of the chain and Leroy stuck his nose out.

"What do you want?"

"I want to talk to your dad."

"He isn't here."

Angela frowned. Technically, in the state of Colorado, it was legal—if ill-advised—to leave a nine-year-old home alone. Guidelines recommended age twelve, but without evidence of endangerment, you could actually leave a six-year-old to fend for himself. Here there were no hard and fast rules. Still, in her mind, leaving a grieving child alone at home, two days after his mother was murdered, bordered on neglect. "When's your dad coming home?"

Leroy shrugged. "He went to the store."

"And you didn't want to go with him?"

"I like it here."

As a kid, Angela would have felt the same way. "How about I visit with you until he gets back?"

"I'm not supposed to let anyone in."

Good instructions from Dad. Through the crack in the door, she could see that the house was a mess. From the blankets on the couch, glasses on the coffee table, and crumbled bags of chips on the floor, it looked like one or both of them had been camping in the living room the last couple of days. No crime in that. "What if we sit out here, on the front porch?"

Leroy shut the door in her face.

Angela wasn't sure if that meant no or if he intended to come out. She waited for what seemed like a couple of minutes, when he finally opened the door and came out onto the porch, wearing the same clothes he'd worn on the fieldtrip. Did that constitute neglect?

Marching past her, he sat down on the stairs. "What do you want to talk about?"

"I want to know how you're doing," she said, sitting down next to him on the top step. She wasn't quite sure how to approach him. When she was a kid, the thing she had hated the most was when people had talked down to her. She figured her best chance at having a dialogue with Leroy was to treat him like a little adult.

"I'm okay."

"It's got to be hard. Is it just you and your dad here? Do you have any family coming?"

"My aunt, my mom's sister, is coming this afternoon."

Angela hoped that was a good thing. Sometimes family was the last thing you needed. "How's your dad doing?"

"Not great." Leroy looked at her pointedly. "What do you want to ask him about? You're not going to accuse him of doing something to my mom again?"

Angela shook her head. "No. I just need to know where your mom was starting at around midnight last night."

"For a timeline," Leroy said.

Angela scrunched up her nose. "It sounds like you watch a lot of TV."

"You think my mom was murdered, don't you? I mean, one of the first things cops do when they know someone was killed is figure out where they were right before they died. That way, they can figure out who the last person to see them alive was."

"You'd make a good detective."

Leroy shook his head. He bent forward, picked up a small pebble and pitched it into the grass. "I want to be an astronaut."

"Or that," Angela said. She needed to press. "So, was your mom here the night before she died?"

"No." Leroy looked up. "I bet you were hoping I'd say yes, weren't you?"

"That would've made my life easier."

Leroy looked back at the step. "She and my dad were both gone. My dad went out with some of the guys from his work, and my mom said she had something to do. She called Jessy."

Angela took it that "Jessy" was the babysitter. "Does Jessy have a last name?"

Leroy shrugged again. It seemed to be his favorite gesture.

"Do you remember what time either of your parents came home?"

"No. Jessy made me go to bed." Leroy pitched another pebble. "That's all I know until my dad woke me up. By then my mom was already gone."

Chapter 8

Angela sat with Leroy until Ron Henderson came home. When Ron pulled up, he got out of his car, grabbed a handful of grocery bags and charged the steps.

"What are you doing here?" he demanded.

"I came to talk to you."

"This isn't a good time."

Where had she heard that before? Angela ignored him. "Any chance we could talk? Alone."

Ron looked between her and Leroy, and then blew out a breath. "Leroy, take these inside."

The boy shuffled his feet, clearly not wanting to get out of earshot. Angela waited for him to disappear into the house.

"We found your wife's car."

"Where?"

"About a half-mile from where we found her body. It's been towed to the impound lot. Once the CSIs are finished processing the vehicle, someone will call you."

"And make me pay to bail it out."

"Unfortunately, that's how it works." Angela didn't think it was fair, but the county had to cover its costs somehow. "Leroy tells me you were out last night."

"Yeah, so?"

"Mr. Henderson, according to the coroner's preliminary report, your wife died from a blow to the head, a blow that could have been sustained any time after midnight. Do you know if she had any sort of accident or altercation with someone?"

"No."

His answer came too quickly. Angela waited. Something else she had learned from Ian. The person with something to hide will either fall silent, or they'll fill the quiet with their version of the truth.

Henderson ran his hands through his hair and blew out another breath. "Look," he said. "Sheila and I were having some problems. Don't get me wrong, I loved my wife, but..."

Angela tried looking sympathetic. "Her friend, Patty, told me she thought you were seeing someone."

A flash of panic crossed Henderson's face and he turned toward his car. Angela followed him down the steps.

"She says you were seeing one of your co-workers. Is that true?" Angela found it hard to stomach a man who fooled around on his wife. She worked hard to give him the benefit of the doubt.

"No." He looked Angela square in the eyes. "Last night, I was out with colleagues. Sheila was angry. She said if I was going out, so was she. She hired a babysitter. She was still out when I got home. She must have come home late and slept in the guest room, because I didn't see her until she was leaving at 5:00 a.m."

"I need the name of the bar, and a list of your colleagues who were there," Angela said.

Henderson narrowed his eyes. "Blame the husband. That's what cops always do. Well, I didn't kill my wife."

That's what they all say. "It's routine, Mr. Henderson. My job requires that I document your wife's final hours, which means accounting for the people she lives with."

"Garcia's. I was there until just before closing."

Angela wrote down the name. For some reason, it rang a bell. "And the names of the people you were with?"

"I'm not dragging anybody else into this." Henderson picked up the last of the grocery bags in the car and slammed the door. "Are we done here?"

"Just one last question, what's the name of your babysitter?"

"Jessy Martinez."

The name sounded familiar. "Ken Martinez's daughter?"

"The same, only she lives with her mother about two blocks over."

"Thanks, Mr. Henderson. We'll be in touch about the car. I'm really sorry for your loss." It sounded condescending.

She watched him stomp up his front walk, and then she climbed into her truck. The next step was obvious. She needed to talk to Jessy.

A quick search turned up an address for Maria Martinez, two blocks over. Angela decided to make a cold call at the residence, and turned the key in the ignition. In route she phoned Deputy Tanner, relieved not to have to deal with Sykes. He had stayed true to his word and focused on the other homicide case, leaving this one to her. She asked Tanner to arrange for a talk with Ken Martinez, told him she needed forty-five minutes, and asked him to text her specifics.

Jessy and her mom lived in a blue, multi-level house with a two car garage, front steps, and a small porch, just like every other house in the subdivision. Climbing the steps to ring the doorbell, Angela noticed a beat up Chevy parked in the driveway. Someone appeared to be home.

Angela rang the doorbell and waited. When no one responded, she rang the doorbell again, and then banged the front door knocker.

"Coming," someone yelled. Angela heard pounding on the stairs, and then the door opened to reveal a teenage girl with an unruly mop of dark hair twisted up in a ponytail.

"Who is it, darling?" called a woman from upstairs.

"I don't know," the girl shouted back. She looked at Angela. "Who are you?"

"Agent Angela Dimato. U.S. Fish and Wildlife."

The girl looked confused, and then the realization struck. "You're here about Mrs. Henderson's murder, aren't you? That's so sad."

"I'm here about her death. The cause is still under investigation."

A woman wearing blue jeans and a t-shirt, and who looked like an older version of Jessy, came down the stairs. "What's this about?"

Angela introduced herself again. "I just need to ask Jessy a couple of questions."

"Like what?" the older woman asked.

"Mom, it's fine," Jessy said. "Shoot."

"When was the last time you saw Mrs. Henderson?"

"Just after I got there. She called and asked if I could watch the monster for a couple of hours. I said sure. I can always use the money."

"So you weren't there when she got back home?"

"Nah, Mr. Henderson came in around 2:30 a.m. He paid me and let me go home."

"I told her when she left that I didn't want her staying out past 1:00 a.m.," Maria Martinez said. "That's plenty late for a young girl to babysit."

"Mom, just leave it."

Clearly, mother and daughter didn't see eye-to-eye.

"Did Mrs. Henderson tell you where she was going?" Angela asked.

"Nah, well, wait. She said she was going to meet Mr. Henderson somewhere. I was kind of surprised when he came home without her, but it's none of my business."

"They're usually pretty good about getting back on time," Maria said. "It surprised me that they kept Jessy so late."

From the expression on Jessy's face, Angela figured the girl never told them about her curfew. "Thanks."

"Sure thing." Jessy nodded and bounded away. Maria started to close the door, when Angela thought to ask her about her ex.

"One more thing?"

"Yes?" Maria seemed wary.

"What can you tell me about the relationship between Sheila Henderson and your ex-husband? I hear they'd had a falling out."

"That woman may have cost our Kenny a scholarship opportunity. He is a star soccer player, and now the school district has suspended all play because of her stupid lawsuit. They won't let the kids on the field until there's a ruling in the case and some decision has been made about how to repair the soccer fields. If Kenny can't play, who will recruit him?"

"And that made your ex-husband mad."

"It made me mad, too. It made a lot of us mad."

"But not everyone made threats. According to at least one person, Mr. Martinez got pretty verbal."

"He said she would be sorry, that he'd make her pay for what she done. It's what people say when they're pissed off."

Angela had to admit, a lot of people threatened to kill someone with no intention of every following through. Unfortunately, this time there was a victim. "Do you think Ken would've hurt her? He has a record for violence."

Maria stepped outside and pulled the door shut. "That happened a long time ago," she said, keeping her voice low. "Ken was barely twenty-one. Some guy was hitting on me in the bar and got a little physical, if you know what I mean. Ken punched him and broke the guy's nose. The guy had it coming."

"Sounds like it," Angela said. Defending his wife, or future wife's honor, was a far cry from most men who were prone to violence. "Just one more question. With the bad blood between your families, why did you let Jessy babysit for the Henderson's?"

"I tried to stay out of it. What's going on is between Ken and Sheila," Maria said, pushing open the door. "Why should Jessy pay the price for that?"

Angela thanked Maria again and went back to the truck. Checking her phone, she found a text from Tanner. He'd arranged to meet Ken Martinez at his house at 6:00 p.m. after he finished his shift. That gave her just over an hour to grab something to eat.

She pulled into La Casa Del Ray, figuring she'd have time to grab a burrito. The parking lot was packed, but she managed to find one spot in the back. Her stomach growled as she walked around to the front door. She hadn't eaten anything all day, except for half of a blueberry muffin at Patty Litchfield's house. Stepping inside made her wish she'd skipped supper.

Sykes was seating alone at a table for two near the door, and waved her over. "Join me."

"Thanks, but I can wait."

"Don't be ridiculous, Angel. Where is it written two colleagues can't share a meal?"

"I've actually lost my appetite."

A slow grin lit up his face, and Angela suddenly felt weak at the knees. She couldn't deny the attraction. Tall and good-looking, he could be as charming as he could be ruthless. "A wolf in sheep's clothing," as the saying went.

As with all animals, do not show fear.

"Sit," he ordered, signaling to the waitress. "I want to hear about the case."

Angela pulled out the chair and sat down. "I thought you weren't interested."

"I'm just curious how it's going. Indulge me."

He was an indulgence she could little afford. Ordering a pork burrito and a diet coke, she gave him an abbreviated version of what she'd discovered to date. She didn't tell him about finding the feather or share any of her theories relating to the eagles. When they were dating, he liked to tease her, calling her a Defender of Wildlife, like she was some Marvel superhero. She chafed at how she'd once thought it endearing, until she realized what little credence he gave to her job as an investigator.

"Sounds like you've got some leads to follow up on."

"What's with you, Sykes?"

He flashed a grin. "What do you mean?"

Angela sat back in her chair. "It's not like you to care anything about my work."

The waitress showed up with her meal, and Angela waited for her to walk away. Once she did, Sykes beat her to the punch.

"The truth is, I've missed you, Angel."

Angela doubted the veracity of his statement, and the little voice in her head was screaming. If he was interested in Henderson's death, it was either because he wanted credit when she solved the case or because he'd come around to the idea that Henderson's death was somehow connected to the case he was working.

"Are you sure it's not because I'm investigating a homicide?"

"A possible homicide," he parried, scooping up a chip full of salsa. "When it becomes a true murder investigation, you know you'll be coming to me for some help."

Chapter 9

After leaving Sykes sitting alone at the table with her untouched burrito, it had taken Angela a few minutes to get her emotions under control. She'd only loved two men in her life and both times she'd been fooled into believing she was someone special, only to have her heart broken. The first had cheated on her with her college roommate; the second had turned out to be a narcissistic scumbag.

Why am I attracted to such losers? she wondered. And where was the little voice in her head when it came to matters of the heart?

Putting the truck into gear, she popped the clutch and headed for the subdivision where Ken Martinez lived. The neighborhood looked shabby compared to his ex-wife's, though she still thought he may have gotten the better end of the divorce. While the ranch-style houses were smaller and more tightly packed together, here the kids rode their bicycles up and down the streets and families were out in their yards. It reminded Angela of the neighborhood she'd grown up in, where everyone knew your business and helped keep you out of trouble.

Tanner was waiting, and climbed out of his vehicle when Angela parked behind him.

"He's home," the deputy said. "He pulled into his drive about five minutes ago. He knows we're out here."

"Why wouldn't he? We made an appointment," she said, leading the way up the paving stones that cut through a postage stamp-sized yard. "We're not here to arrest him, Tanner. We're just going to ask him a few questions."

"Gotcha."

Martinez opened his front door before Angela and Tanner reached the end of the walk.

"What's this about?" he asked, blocking their entry.

"Sheila Henderson," Angela said.

"What's that bitch up to now?"

"She's dead," Tanner said.

Angela watched the color leave Martinez's face. The man hadn't known. "She was found dead yesterday morning," she said. "We hear you had some trouble with her."

"Who didn't?" Martinez said. "Come on in. We can go out in the back." He led the way through a small, neat house to a small, neatly trimmed backyard. Angela noticed a bird feeder hanging from the limb of the large cottonwood that shaded the grass. Small gray birds swamped the feeder and decorated the branches of the shrubbery, keeping a determined red squirrel at bay. Four chairs lined a concrete patio. He gestured for them to sit down.

"Mr. Martinez, when was the last time you saw Sheila Henderson?" Angela asked.

"A week or so ago. We weren't friends."

"That sounds like an understatement," Tanner said. "People say you threatened her."

Martinez looked at the deputy. "I didn't hurt her, if that's what you think. She made trouble for my boy. She made trouble for a lot of people."

"Because of the soccer program?" Angela asked.

"Because of a lot of things. That woman liked to sue people. She was always looking for an angle to get what she wanted."

Angela took out her notebook. "Besides you, who else was she suing?"

"Who hadn't she sued might be a better question. She sued her homeowner's association for allowing one of her neighbors to paint their house an unauthorized shade of blue. She sued her landscape architect for planting trees in her yard that died. She sued some kid for rear-ending her car and wanted his insurance company to pay her ten thousand dollars. The woman was a sleazy lawyer's wet dream."

"So you admit she was a nuisance, someone you'd just as soon be rid of?" Tanner said.

Angela wanted to gag him. Antagonizing a suspect wouldn't get them the answers they wanted. "What Deputy Tanner means"

"I know what he means. I'll admit she was a pain, but that doesn't mean I did anything to her." He looked at Angela. "Do I need a lawyer?"

"Deputy Tanner isn't accusing you of harming her, Mr. Martinez," Angela said.

Tanner shrugged, as if to say maybe he was, maybe he wasn't.

Martinez kept his focus on Angela. "What time did you say she was murdered?"

"We didn't," Tanner said. "How do you know she was murdered?"

Martinez glared at the deputy. "You said she was dead, so she must have been killed. Why else would you come here asking questions?"

"Mr. Martinez, where were you two nights ago?" Angela asked.

"Work," he answered. "I worked a double shift. The night shift super called in, so I was at work from eleven until 8:00 a.m. You can verify with the general manager."

"You can bet on it," Tanner said.

"Mr. Martinez, do you know the names of anyone else who might have wanted to harm Sheila Henderson?" Angela asked.

"You might try talking to her husband."

"Why's that?"

"Those two were not getting along. Sheila told everyone who would listen that she thought he was having an affair. I think she was hoping someone would confirm her suspicions and give her a name." Martinez pushed out of his chair. "Are we about finished? I haven't eaten yet, and I haven't slept much for a couple of days. I'd like to get myself some dinner and hit the hay."

There was nothing to do but follow him to the door. After Martinez showed them out, Angela stormed across the street to Tanner's patrol car.

She managed to keep her mouth shut until they were both seated inside, then she turned on the deputy. "What the heck was that, Tanner? We were here to ask questions, not to accuse him of anything. He might have given us more answers if you'd been more civil."

"He has motive," the deputy said. "I was trying to smoke him out."

"You almost forced him to lawyer up."

"I figured maybe if I pushed him a little, he would tip his hand."

Angela shook her head. "My old partner used to say, 'If you push too hard, people clam up.'" She stared hard at Tanner. "Next time you could try soft-pedaling it just a little?"

He shrugged. "And if that doesn't work?"

"Then you can break his arm." She gave him an extra big smile to let him know she was joking. "Seriously, where's the harm?"

"Fine."

"Great." This time her smile was genuine. "We still need to check his alibi."

"Consider it done." Tanner placed the call and the Walmart manager confirmed that Martinez had worked the night shift. There were twelve guys who could attest to the fact he was there all night and never left the building.

"Just to be sure, we should pull the surveillance tapes." Angela said. Employees and co-workers could be pretty loyal sometimes, and the tapes would show if Martinez had slipped out at any time during his shift.

"If it's not him, who else is on the list? The husband?"

"He's one," Angela said. They hadn't been able to rule him out. They still needed to verify his whereabouts that evening and who he was with, which meant a stop at Garcia's. There was also the alleged girlfriend to interview, and they needed to find out where Sheila Henderson had gone on the night she was murdered.

Angela suddenly realized she was starving. Thanks to her run-in with Sykes, she'd never had lunch. At Garcia's, she could kill two birds with one stone. "Do you feel like a burger, Tanner?"

"I suppose I could eat. Why? You got something in mind?"

"Yeah. Henderson said he was at Garcia's with colleagues until just before closing time. I hear they make a mean slider."

Chapter 10

Garcia's was located in a strip mall off of Quebec St. and 58th, and the parking lot was packed. Most of the vehicles were pickups or beat up vans, with one or two lowriders tucked in. Happy Hour appeared to be in full swing. The music was so loud that the walls of the building appeared to pulse, and Angela could feel the bass vibrate through the asphalt in the parking lot.

She scanned the console of the patrol car. "Do you have any earplugs in here?"

"Man up," Tanner said.

The customers in the parking lot eyed the two of them warily as they walked from the parking lot to the front door. Tanner reached for the handle.

"Allow me," he said.

"This isn't a date."

"I know, but what's wrong with showing some manners? You're too old for me anyway."

Angela bristled at the comment. He was what, five years younger than she was? Still, she let him open the door. Not because she was his elder, but beauty before brawn.

Once inside, the blare of the country-western band dissuaded all conversation. She stood and allowed her eyes to adjust to the dimly lit room, then scanned the interior. It looked like the type of place that attracted a blue-collar drinking crowd. Chairs were haphazardly pulled up to tables covered with pitchers, glasses, and appetizer plates. The dance floor was packed.

Working their way over to the long wooden bar, Tanner commandeered two empty barstools and ordered a beer. She was surprised when the bartender didn't card the deputy, but asked to see her ID.

"Really?" She showed him her license, and then ordered a Diet Coke and a burger. "Heavy on the blue cheese, and add some bacon."

"You got it." The bartender pointed to Tanner. "How about you?"

Tanner ordered a flauta.

"Busy in here today," Angela said when the bartender returned with her drink.

"Always." He set down her glass and Tanner's beer. "The food and water will be up in a few minutes."

"No rush," she said, "but we need to ask you some questions."

The bartender made a face. A waitress down at the other end was signaling to him, and at least three customers were holding out empty beer glasses. "You're going to have to wait."

"No problem." Angela glanced over at Tanner. He was seated, but bopping his feet along to the beat.

He gestured toward the band. "They're not bad."

Angela scanned the bar crowd while they waited for the food to arrive. The crowd was mostly white and Hispanic. The type of place an engineer and his crew might come. The type of place a person could let loose after a hard day on the job. Maybe she'd stop in on her next day off.

Once the food arrived, Angela focused all her attention on the burger at hand. As she mopped up the ketchup with her last fry, the bartender materialized.

"I've got a few minutes if you want to step outside. It's easier to hear and I can have a smoke."

Angela signaled to Tanner.

The sun was setting on the foothills when they reached the parking lot, painting the sky a deep red and dropping the temperature to a comfortable level.

The bartender lit a cigarette. "So what is it you want to know?"

Angela produced a picture of Ron Henderson. "Do you remember seeing this guy in here with a group of colleagues two nights ago?"

"I remember the dude, but I don't know if I'd call the woman he was with a colleague."

That supported Patty's allegations that he was seeing someone. "Can you describe her?"

"Let me clarify. The dude came in with a group, but the rest of them split pretty fast. Then a woman joined him. They stayed until nearly 1:30 a.m. I remember the time because it was last call. The dude wanted to go, but the chick wanted another drink. I didn't get out of here until 2:00 a.m. or so, and then the cops had me back here early that morning."

"What for?" Tanner asked.

Angela tamped down her annoyance at his veering off track. "Wait, first tell me. What did the woman look like?"

The bartender answered Tanner's question first. "Two guys were gunned down in our parking lot."

Sykes's case! Ever since Sykes had wanted to know what she'd turned up on Sheila's murder, Angela's little voice had been suggesting that the murders were connected.

"What did the detectives want from you?" Tanner asked.

The bartender took another drag off his cigarette. "They showed me a couple of pictures of the guys and asked for the bar's surveillance tapes. They think one of the dudes left his car here the night before."

"Did you recognize either of the men?" Angela asked, deciding she could come back to the woman.

"Nah. The place was crowded that night and I had some company at the bar that was holding my attention, if you get my drift."

"Then how do you remember Henderson and the woman he was with?" Angela asked.

"Hey, she was all over the dude. I was about to suggest they get a room, when he went out to smoke a cigarette. He came back all flipped out. He sent the chick out the back and he left through the front. I thought it was weird."

"Can you describe the woman he was with?"

"Average. She wasn't bad looking, but she wasn't great either."

"Hair color or eye color?" Tanner asked.

The bartender took one last drag on his cigarette and ground the butt into the asphalt. "She was a brunette. I prefer blondes."

That meant, whoever Ron Henderson was with, it wasn't Sheila. "Can you remember anything else about her?"

"Sorry," the bartender said. "You want to know what someone's drinking, I can tell you that."

"What was she drinking?" Angela asked.

"He ordered beer. She was banging down gin and colas, no ice."

Angela couldn't help but make a face. It matched Tanner's.

"Dude, you'd be surprised at the things people order," the bartender said.

"Thanks," Tanner said, then sarcastically added, "dude."

The bartender didn't notice, but it made Angela smile.

Chapter 11

It was dark by the time Angela and the deputy got back to her truck, but they had come up with a game plan. The next morning, Tanner was going to check the surveillance tapes at the Walmart in the morning, while she went to see the alleged girlfriend, Ellie Parker.

After breakfast, Angela called Patty Litchfield before heading out to the Parker residence. If the she were really Shelia's best friend, it was possible she might know where Shelia had gone the night before she was murdered.

Patty picked up on the first ring. Angela identified herself. The answer to her question was no.

Ellie Parker and her husband lived in the Reunion neighborhood of Commerce City—a little north and east of the area where the Henderson's lived. The houses looked the same, just larger and newer, with bigger yards. Angela had called ahead, so Ellie was expecting her.

"You must be Agent Dimato," she said, greeting Angela at the door. The woman was tall, with dark hair pulled back into a low bun and dark eyes circled with eyeliner. Angela wouldn't have called her beautiful. Statuesque seemed a more accurate descriptor.

"Thanks for making time to see me this morning."

"It's no trouble," Ellie said, leading the way into a formal living room area with stiff-backed chairs and wall-to-wall bookcases on three sides. While the vibe said friendly, the room was shy of being welcoming. At least the chairs weren't covered in plastic.

Before they could sit, the phone rang.

"I need to get this," Ellie said, gesturing toward a straight-backed chair. "Have a seat. I'll be right back."

Instead of sitting down, Angela walked over to the bookcases. Most of the shelves were filled with leather bound editions of the Law Review, which made sense since her husband was an attorney. In addition, she spotted a few mystery and romance novels and several travel guides. One of two of the other shelves held framed photographs and artifacts. The most interesting ones were a grouping of Indian artifacts beside two framed photographs—one of a handsome Native American and one of a young boy.

"That's our son," Ellie said, wrapping her arms tightly around her chest.

Angela hadn't seen any mention of children in Ellie's profile. "How old is he?"

"He would be eight." Her hand reached toward the picture as if wanting to caress the child's face, then her expression hardened. "He died shortly after that picture was taken."

Angela wasn't sure what to say. Any words would be small by comparison to the grief etched into Ellie's face. "I'm sorry."

"He developed leukemia and I've never been able to have any more children, though I tried."

Her use of the word "I" struck Angela as odd. Hoping to steer the interview back on more solid footing, she pointed to the other photo. "Who is this?"

Ellie set down the picture of her son, and brightened slightly when she touched the picture of the older man. "That is a picture of my husband's great-great-great-grandfather, Quanah Parker."

"Your husband is Native American?"

"He is, though you would never know it. We discovered it when Ethan was asked to write a genealogy report. The kids were asked to go back as many generations as they could, so I started looking through old albums." Ellie grew more animated as she talked, and Angela found her enthusiasm infectious.

"Do you know much about your family history?" Ellie asked.

"I know I'm Italian. My father was a Dimato, my mother a Cabello. I get it from both sides."

"Are you Catholic?"

Angela was surprised by the personal question. "Yes, for generations."

"Me, too," Ellie said. "I think that's why I find my husband's family so interesting." She walked over to where Angela stood and pointed to a large carved box sitting on the floor beside a small drum. "This contains some religious items that have been passed down to Sam. It's an old peyote box that belonged to Quanah Parker. Are you at all familiar with him?"

"Wasn't he a Comanche chief?" Angela must have gotten it right because Ellie lit up.

"The last free Comanche chief. He was a famous warrior, and led his people in battle against the white man and then led them to surrender at Fort Sill."

If Angela remembered her history, he also negotiated land settlements for his people that later generated large income through grazing leases. "Wasn't his mother white?"

Ellie nodded. "Cynthia Ann Parker. She was captured during a Comanche raid when she was nine years-old. She grew up among the Indians and fell in love with Chief Peta Noconi. They had three children. Quanah was the oldest. When he was still a young boy, his mother was re-captured by Texas Rangers. History says she begged to be returned to the Comanche, and even tried escaping, but she was forced to live with her white relatives and eventually died of a broken heart. Quanah later took her surname in her honor."

"If this box belonged to him, it's a museum piece."

"It definitely is. My husband had it appraised and it's worth thousands. Each box was very individualized."

"May I look inside?"

A look of uncertainty crossed Ellie's face. "These are sacred religious items."

"I can tell they mean a lot to you. Are you Native American, too?"

"Me? No." Ellie shook her head. "I'm of Eastern European descent. Though, spiritually, I feel a connection. You know, Cynthia Parker always considered herself a Comanche."

"Do any of the items inside belonged to her?"

"There's a picture." Ellie seemed to wrestle with herself for a moment, then she suddenly opened the box, took out a photograph of a young white woman in Indian dress and handed it to Angela. "She was beautiful, wasn't she?"

Angela stared at the photograph. "It's remarkable how much you look like her."

"Do you think so?" Ellie was clearly pleased.

"Definitely." Angela wondered just how obsessed Ellie was with her husband's past. She gestured to the box. "Do you mind?"

Again, Ellie hesitated. "Just don't touch anything."

"Not a problem."

While Ellie held it open, Angela peered into the box. Inside were a feather fan, a gourd rattle and a wooden stick with carvings that matched the rattle. The items were decorated with intricate beading. Four bald eagle tail feathers, two broken, hung from beading on the wooden rattle, while the fan was made of ten perfect bald eagle wing feathers bound together by hemp rope. Smudged with the resin and ash of century old fire, Angela could tell they were old.

In addition to the larger items, there were smaller, personal artifacts as well—a rosary, arrowheads, several Indian head pennies, and a small pearl stickpin.

Angela had seen similar artifacts come into the repository, but nothing as spectacular as these. "They're remarkable."

"According to history, it was Quanah Parker who brought the peyote ceremony to the Numinu, the people. He and the men would gather in a tent, where there was an altar for the peyote button. Each man would bring his own peyote set, along with a drum. They would gather in a semi-circle around Father Peyote, and then they would drum and rattle and pray. And drink peyote tea and smoke hand-rolled cigarettes, of course. The fans were used to waft their prayers to the heavens. In the morning, the women would feed the men a feast and then they would all go home until the next time."

Angela handed the picture back to Ellie and watched her gently put it away. "If your husband's interested, we could catalog the contents and date the feathers to verify its authenticity."

"That's a nice offer, but Sam wouldn't be interested. As romantic a notion as I might find it—that he's the son of an Indian chief and I am his princess—he doesn't much care. He finds his heritage interesting and all, but he's way too busy to give it much thought." Ellie set the box down and again gestured at the grouping of chairs. "Now, what is it you wanted to see me about?"

Angela perched on the edge of her seat and decided to get right to the point. "I'm investigating the death of Sheila Henderson, and it's been suggested by someone close to the investigation that you're friendly with the deceased's husband, Ron."

"We work together if that's what you mean."

Angela tried to think of a delicate way to broach the subject of cheating on one's spouse and sleeping with another woman's husband. "Closer. We've been told that you and Mr. Henderson are intimately involved."

Ellie reared back in her chair. "Are you accusing me of having an affair with Ron?"

Angela pursed her lips. "I'm asking you if it's true."

"No. That's absurd. Who told you that?" Ellie's eyes flashed anger. "Ron would never do that."

"You're right," Angela said. "It was someone else who told us."

"Someone from my office?"

Angela leaned forward. "Why would you ask that?"

Ellie stood and paced the length of the room. "I'm a woman working a man's job. A number of my co-workers still believe the only way a woman could climb the ladder as fast as I have is by sleeping with the boss. Well, it's not true."

"So you're denying you and Ron have a special friendship."

"Not at all. He's been a great mentor, and friend. We spend a lot of time together, just not in the way you're suggesting." She tucked back a stray lock of hair. "I am a happily married woman. I love my work. I'm a dedicated engineer. And I want to know who slandered my name."

Angela chose a different tack. "Were you with Ron at Garcia's bar two nights ago?"

Ellie frowned. "Early in the evening, along with three other co-workers. We were celebrating the completion of one of the bridges. We stopped there for a beer."

"Who else was with you?"

Ellie rattled off five names, including hers and Ron's.

"How long did you stay?"

"I don't know. I left early, before dinner. Ron and a couple of the guys were still there. You can ask them if you don't believe me."

"And you came straight home?"

"Yes. It was getting late, and I knew my husband would be wondering where I was."

Chapter 12

Wrapping up with Ellie, Angela was ten minutes late meeting Tanner. Winding her way through the desks in the squad room, she found him hunched over his computer watching a video replay.

"Anything?" she asked.

"Oh, yeah," he said, hitting the rewind button. "Check this out."

He hit play again and the image of the Walmart parking lot appeared. The picture was grainy, but it showed a clear shot of a gray 4Runner pulling into a parking space with Sheila Henderson climbing out from behind the wheel, and then disappearing into the store.

"It doesn't prove that she saw Ken Martinez," Angela said.

"Keep watching." Tanner hit the fast forward button, and then hit play again. This time there was a picture of Sheila exiting the store with Martinez behind her. They appeared to exchange words, before he went back inside and Sheila climbed into her car and drove away.

Martinez had lied to them.

"What time was that?" Angela asked.

"By the log, about 1:00 a.m."

Within the time frame of the head injury. "It looks like we'll need to talk with Martinez again."

"Agreed." Tanner reached for a stack of papers on his desk. "But that's not all I discovered. I found something else while I was poking around this morning. Remember how Martinez said that the vic was always suing people. I discovered that she has more than one lawsuit filed against the city." He held out the papers. "Take a look."

Angela took the pages and pulled up an empty chair. She didn't have to read far to realize they had just opened up their suspect pool.

A year ago, Sheila had filed a lawsuit against Commerce City and the U.S. Army. According to the document in Angela's hands, the woman claimed to hold the original deed to one hundred sixty acres of Rocky Mountain Arsenal land; acreage later annexed by Commerce City. Sheila asserted that the documentation she held proved that her family was never compensated for the land taken by the U.S. Army in 1942. She claimed that, as the Henderson's sole heir, she was entitled to ownership and use of the land and/or payment and interest for the acreage in question. She was seeking in excess of three million dollars.

Angela flipped the page and found another item of interest. In addition to Commerce City, one individual had recently been added to the suit; someone against whom Sheila was seeking personal damages— Carl Leeds, the mayor of Commerce City.

Angela looked up. "Isn't Carl Leeds up for reelection?"

"Next year," Tanner said. "Is it even legal to sue the government?"

"I would imagine there are liability limits, and she'd need a damn good attorney, but I think it's possible." Angela turned to the back page. When she found the attorney's name, she let out a whistle. "Guess who's listed as Sheila's attorney?"

"I'm guessing it's someone we know."

"Samuel Parker."

"The mistress's husband?"

Angela set the papers down on the corner of his desk. "For the record, Ellie Parker claims that's a lie. She vehemently denies having any sort of illicit relationship with Ron. She did admit to being at Garcia's that night, but says she left before all of her co-workers did. We'll need to verify that."

"Can do," Tanner said. "But first, I'm going to head over to Walmart to talk to Martinez."

Angela stood and pushed back the chair. "I have to stop by the repository and file the paperwork with the DOI." Plus Wayne was probably having a fit that she hadn't shown up to work already. The report was due before noon. "Let me know what Martinez says. I'll schedule meetings with the mayor and Parker for later this afternoon and let you know the times. Maybe we can head by Garcia's afterwards?"

"Sounds like a plan."

It was close to 11:30 a.m. by the time Angela reached the warehouse, and most of the staff was clocked out for lunch. It took her fifteen minutes to file the paperwork with the DOI, and nearly double the time on the phone to arrange meetings with Parker and Leeds. Parker could meet with them at 3:00 p.m., but Leeds was tied up until 5:00 p.m.

Angela texted Tanner the times, checked in with Wayne, and then headed downstairs to the main area of the repository to see what new cases had come in during the past few days. She had just reached the warehouse floor, when Sykes walked through the door.

"Just the person I wanted to see," he said.

"I can't say the feeling is mutual. What do you want?" It struck her that Sykes might be here about Sheila Henderson. The coroner's ruling of blunt force trauma made her death a homicide. Had Adams County reassigned him the murder?

"Don't look so scared, Angel. I'm not here to commandeer your case. I'm here about the double shooting and homicide I've been working. I need you to take a look at something."

That's when Angela noticed the large brown bag he gripped in his hand. Taking it, she gingerly opened the sack. Inside was a jumbled mass of eagle feathers.

Sadness and anger coursed through her. Her supposition was right. Her little voice was batting a thousand. Something had happened to one of the nesting pair. Sheila must have witnessed it and paid the ultimate price.

Moving to a steel table, she dumped out the contents of the bag and sorted them into order. All in all, she counted thirty-nine feathers. One shy of a full bird. Her stomach grew queasy. "Where did you find these?"

"On the back seat of my victim's car. What am I looking at here?"

"Eagle feathers. You're one shy. Except, I know where it is. Wayne and I found a feather out by the eyrie yesterday. I'll bet a hundred bucks it matches these."

"The eyrie?"

"The eagles' nest." It felt good knowing something he didn't. "Hold on a minute while I retrieve the other feather." Angela pounded up the stairs, grabbed the feather off of her desk and returned, slipping it into the mix. It was a perfect match. There was no doubt it belonged to the same bird, and she had no doubt that Sheila Henderson died because of something to do with the death of this eagle.

Sykes scratched his head. "You're sure it fits?"

"Positive."

"But wouldn't almost any feather fit?"

"No. A bird's wing and tail feathers have a certain shape. The type, size, and age of a bird determine the shape, length, and color of the feathers. There's a lot of variation. This feather is a clearly a perfect match. We could run a DNA test if you like"

"Nah, that won't be necessary." Sykes eyed her like she was crazy. "So what in the heck would my guys be doing with a bag of feathers?"

"Is either one Native American?"

Sykes shrugged. "Let's say yes, for the sake of argument."

"Well then, it's possible they planned to use them for religious purposes or to make traditional costumes. Or maybe they just planned to sell them. Eagle feathers are worth a lot on the black market."

"Except it's not against the law for them to have them if they're Native Americans."

"That's not necessarily true. It depends on the age of the feathers, and they would still need to apply for a permit if they planned on killing a bird. Without proper authorization, possession of these feathers constitutes a violation of the Bald Eagle Act and the Migratory Bird Treaty. Plus they could be charged under the Lacey Act. We're talking about felony charges and fines up to $250K."

Sykes whistled.

Angela decided now was as good a time as any to float her theory about their cases. "Has it occurred to you that maybe the shootings and Sheila Henderson's murder are connected?"

"What makes you say that?"

"The single feather was found in an area where Sheila had been just before her death. Based on these," she gestured to the feathers, "and the tire tracks, I think it's possible she came in contact with your victims."

"You can't be sure of that."

"You're guys are missing a feather that was found in the same area where Sheila parked her car just before she died."

"Hell, my guys could have dropped it long before she showed up."

"Or maybe she caught them in the act."

"So they killed her, and then dumped her body in the middle of prairie dog town, dumped her car, and just happened to leave you a clue?"

"Most criminals aren't rocket scientists."

"True, but face it, Angel, your victim died from a blow to the noggin, probably sustained during the car crash. Both of my guys had weapons on them. And so, I might add, did the guy who shot 'em. If your victim caught those bozos out there with the bird, why didn't they shoot her?"

"Maybe they couldn't risk firing a weapon. Rangers patrol out there all of the time. Or maybe the blow to her head incapacitated her. Maybe they thought she was dead and they didn't think there was any need." Angela knew she was grasping at straws. "All I know is, if Sheila witnessed those men killing the bird, they easily might have murdered her to keep her quiet. Did either of the men have a record?"

"I get where you're going with this, but I'm not buying it, Angel."

"Yes or no."

"Yes, both men have long rap sheets, and a felony charge would tag them both as habitual offenders. They could both have been looking at a lifetime in prison."

"There's your motive."

"Except one is already dead and the other's already looking at life in prison. Feather possession charges aside, I've got him on illegal drug possession, illegal possession of firearms, and unlawful weapons discharge. That's enough to put him inside and throw away the key." Sykes picked up a feather and twirled it. "The bottom line is you can't even tie your dead woman to the bird."

His dismissiveness annoyed her.

"I can by proximity," she countered.

"Circumstantial at best, Angel. It's not good enough." Sykes set the feather back down. "You show me a rock solid connection between my two guys and the dead woman, and I'll consider your theories. But right now, even if the feather had been found in her possession, any lousy attorney could say that she picked it up off the ground. Especially because she was near the—what did you call it—eyrie. And for that matter, without the carcass, who's to say that your gal and my guys didn't just find all these feathers?" He snapped his fingers. "Or wait, maybe your gal sold them to my guys and she's the shooter?"

"You don't really believe that, do you?"

He drew a deep breath and locked eyes with her. "No. But, until you find me a carcass that I can connect to my vics, I'm going to leave you holding the bag." He chuckled at his own joke, and then pointed to feathers. "So what happens to these now?"

Angela pulled the feather she'd added out of the pile and set it off to one side, then replaced the feather Sykes had removed from the display on the tray. Like it or not, he was doing his job. Now she needed to do hers.

"I'll tag the ones you brought in and hold them as evidence," Angela said. "You did the right thing, bringing them here. I'll need the name of the person or persons you found in possession of the feathers. I'll run them against the database and see either one has the right to be in possession."

"The driver was Donny Smith. He's dead. His passenger suffered a gunshot wound and is in critical condition. I have no way of knowing who the bag belonged to. The feathers were found in the back seat. If we're lucky, the passenger will live long enough to tell us something."

"Who was the car registered to?" Technically, she could charge the owner.

"The dead driver."

"What about witnesses?"

"A few folks told me the shooter took off on foot, but not one of them can give me an accurate description. The only consensus was that he was slight of build and was carrying a gun. We canvased the area, checked all the surveillance tapes, and turned up nothing."

Garcia's. Maybe the connection between Sheila and Sykes's victims wasn't the Refuge, or the bird. Maybe it was the bar. "The bartender at

Garcia's told me you confiscated the surveillance video."

"Yeah, so...?"

"I'd like to look at it."

"What for?"

She opted for the straight answer, omitting any additional theories. "Sheila Henderson's husband, Ron, was the last person to see her alive. We have witnesses that put him inside Garcia's the night before his wife's body was discovered. According to the bartender, he was there with a woman and they were very friendly. Then just before last call, Ron went outside for a smoke. He must have seen something in the parking lot that spooked him. The bartender said he was really jumpy when he came back in, and that a few minutes later he sent his mystery woman out through the back while he left through the front."

"And you're hoping to ID this nameless female."

"If possible. At the very least, it would be nice to know what spooked the husband so badly that he cut his date short." While Angela was at it, she intended to check out the timeline on Sykes's victims, too, but Sykes didn't need to know that. "Are the tapes any good?"

"Crystal clear. One of my vics parked his car at the backend of the lot and got into the other vic's car about 9:00 p.m. They drove off and didn't come back until just after 7:00 a.m., just in time to get shot."

Even the timing dovetailed—provided Ron Henderson was telling the truth about when Sheila left home that morning. If she had gone straight out to the Refuge, and the two men were out there, they could have easily crossed paths.

Angela glanced at the clock. Her appointment!

"Thanks for bringing these by," she said. Picking up a camera, she snapped several photos of the feathers. "Is it okay if I stop by the office tomorrow to look at the surveillance tapes?"

"Sure, what the heck? I'll have them loaded up on the computer, just in case I'm out. Tanner can access them for you. I can't let you have the originals. Chain of custody, and all that."

"Not a problem." All she wanted to do was fill in the time gaps.

Sykes rapped his knuckles against the steep table, signaling he was going to take off. "Anything else you need from me?"

"Just the name of the other victim in your case."

Sykes chuckled. "And here I thought I might get away clean."

"I just want to check his name against the Native American database. If neither one of your victims is registered and allowed to be in possession of the feathers, it makes filing charges that much easier."

"You're like a dog with a bone."

Angela didn't mind the analogy. "His name."

"Patrick Begay. But you know you'll never be able to make it stick. Not if you can't prove which perp they belong to."

"You have a point," she said, transferring the feathers to a locked cabinet. "How about a chance to talk with him?"

"Sure, Angel. But right now he has a breathing tube shoved down his throat. You're going to have to stand in line."

Chapter 13

The law offices of Parker & Hall were located on the third floor of a ten-story high-rise off of Quebec, just south of I-70, across from a new upscale development in the old Stapleton area. The attorney's names were stenciled in white on the glass door and a perky receptionist manned the front desk.

"May I help you?"

Angela handed her a card. "Special Agent Angela Dimato of U.S. Fish and Wildlife and Deputy Tanner from Adams County Sheriff's department. We're here to see Sam Parker."

"Have a seat," the receptionist said. "I'll let him know you're here."

Angela sat opposite Tanner in a large, plush, oversized chair that made her feel trapped. The color scheme was pale gray. Plush sofas and chairs were strategically placed, while giant John Fielder photographs of Colorado adorned the walls. On the back wall were two large, gilt-framed paintings of two men. The man on the left appeared to be Parker, so the other man had to be Hall.

Parker stared back from the canvas through wide-set eyes that were over high cheek-bones and a long nose. She was struck by his resemblance to the photograph of Quanah Parker back on his bookcase, even though in the painting, his dark hair was cut short and he bore a smile.

"A little ostentatious for my tastes," said a man behind her. "It was my partner's idea."

She turned to find Sam Parker looming over her. At just over six feet, he was an imposing man dressed impeccably in khaki's, a blue oxford shirt opened at the collar, and a charcoal sports coat.

"It's a good likeness," Angela said.

"Thanks. Now, if you'll follow me to my office. "

Angela and Tanner walked behind him to a large corner office that looked out over the city. Clearly it was meant to impress.

He waved them to two chairs. "Now, what can I do for you?"

"We understand that you represented Sheila Henderson in several lawsuits," Angela said. "One against the city, the school district, and Ken Martinez, and one against the City and U.S. Army."

"Both are a matter of public record."

"I take it you know she died," Tanner said.

Parker's gaze sharpened, more hawkish. "Yes."

Angela shifted in her seat. "Mr. Parker, we're trying to find out if anyone might have wanted your client dead. Can you tell us a little more about the lawsuits?"

Parker picked up a pencil from his desk and twirled it in his fingers. "I'm sure you've read the filings."

Angela could tell he was deliberately making this difficult. What Ian would have called playing it close to the vest. "Let's start with the case Sheila brought against the U.S. Army and Commerce City."

Parker balanced the pencil on the end of his index finger. "Sheila holds ownership of one hundred sixty acres of Rocky Mountain Arsenal land. Her family was never properly compensated and the documents of ownership were never turned over. The case is solid."

"How did the government react to the suit?" Angela asked. She doubted they took it well.

"They think it's frivolous." Parker flipped the pencil into the air, caught it firmly in his fist, and then let it roll off the palm of his hand onto his fingertips. "Frankly, Agent Dimato, I don't want to tip my hand to you. Based on your connection to the Refuge and Deputy Tanner's connection to Adams County, I think telling the two of you anything could compromise my ability to use certain information in court."

Tanner leaned forward, his posture threatening. "This is a murder investigation, Mr. Parker. We expect some answers. Don't make me hit you with obstruction charges."

Angela cringed. Parker laughed and flipped the pencil again.

"You've been watching too much crime TV, officer."

"Deputy," Tanner corrected.

Parker lounged back in his chair. "You must understand, Deputy. My obligation is to my client."

"But as we've pointed out," Tanner said, "she's dead."

Parker gripped the front edge of his desk and scooted his chair in. "But her heirs aren't. I've already spoken with her husband about going forward with the case. He's agreed we should pursue it. Unfortunately, I am compelled to protect my client's interest in this matter and I am under no obligation to share any information with you."

"Then I guess we need to speak with your client," Tanner said.

"If Ron will talk with you and wishes to share details of the case, that's his prerogative. Though, be assured, I will advise him against it."

Tanner started to speak, but Angela stopped him. "Fair enough, Parker. What about Sheila's other case, the one against the school district and city regarding the soccer fields?"

"It's in mediation."

"So you're nearing a settlement of some sort. Does she have any other cases pending?"

"That information is confidential."

"And I'll take that as a yes," Angela said, annoyed at his stonewalling.

Tanner pushed to his feet. "This has been a waste of time. You haven't told us anything."

"That's a matter of perspective," Parker said. "I haven't wasted my time, because there is something we need to clarify."

Angela was gripped by a sense of unease. "What's that?"

"You came by my house this morning and spoke with my wife."

"I did." It didn't surprise her that Ellie had told him about the visit.

"From here on out, if you have any questions for my wife, you are to contact me. While she is happy to cooperate, she felt the tone of your conversation was accusatory. Any further conversations will be conducted with either myself or a member of my firm present." Parker stood and handed her a card. "Is that understood?"

Angela knew he was only protecting his wife and client, but she struggled to mask her dislike for the man. His tactics epitomized what she liked least about lawyers—most of them had a kill instinct that rivaled a badger's.

Reaching out, she took the card and tucked it into her pocket. "I'm sure that we'll have more questions, Mr. Parker. Count on my being in touch."

Chapter 14

They arrived early for the meeting at the mayor's office. Here, instead of opulence, the reception area was utilitarian. The walls were painted institutional beige and the floors tiled. Ten-by-twelve photographs of the council members graced one wall, flanked on either side by the U.S. and state of Colorado flags. Cushioned metal chairs formed four columns with a wide center aisle.

Angela strode forward to the curved receptionist's desk, and asked the skinny woman manning the desk if Mayor Leed was in.

The woman looked up and smiled. "He's here and waiting for you."

She picked up the phone and dialed, and Mayor Leed appeared to greet them before she'd replaced the receiver.

"Welcome," he said, waddling down the hall toward them. He dressed the part of a politician, wearing a blue suit with a navy and red barber-pole striped tie. He glad-handed them both in the typical fashion of a politician up for reelection. "I'm pleased to know that you're being thorough about looking into Sheila Henderson's death. That poor woman. She had some issues and made a lot of folks angry, but I was shocked to hear she was murdered."

"The main reason we're here is all those angry folks," Angela said.

Tanner nodded. "We want to know if someone like you had it in for her."

Angela maintained a straight face and studied the mayor's reaction. While there was no question the deputy needed to learn some tact, she was beginning to appreciate the effect his blunt statements had on people.

Mayor Leed seemed visibly shaken. Glancing around the reception area to see who, other than the receptionist, might have overheard their conversation, he gestured for them to follow him down the hallway into a barebones conference room and shut the door.

"She upset a lot of people," he said once they were seated. "But honestly, I don't know anyone, at least not anyone from my office, that wanted her harmed."

"You sure about that?" Tanner asked. "She pointed the finger at you in at least one lawsuit."

The deputy was on a roll.

"Mayor, where do the lawsuits stand?" Angela asked.

Leed wiggled in his chair at the head of the table. His ample body filled the seat and sweat beaded on his tanned forehead. "I take it you know about both of them then?"

Angela nodded.

Leed planted his elbows on the table. Folding his hands together, he leaned in. "At the end of the school year, pending an outcome of an investigation I ordered into the condition of the fields, the city council and school district voted to suspend the Adams County school district's soccer program. As the governing body in Adams County, the city council takes its role as stewards of our community very seriously."

Angela listened to him drone on with the political rhetoric for a moment, and then cut him off with another question. "How did the community react to your suspending the program?"

"Not well. They didn't like the decision one bit. But, as city council members, sometimes we have to make wise, prudent calls in the face of opposition, for the betterment of our citizens."

In other words, the city council couldn't afford to take the risk of another student being injured and another lawsuit being filed.

"Who did it tick off the most?" Tanner asked.

Mayor Leed didn't miss a beat. "Ken Martinez. He claimed that we had caved-in on the soccer issue because of the other litigation. He's threatened to file recall petitions for all the council members, myself included."

"In an election year?" Angela asked.

"Yes. And I won't deny that Sheila Henderson has made it hellish. The condition of our soccer fields is a minor problem when compared with the real issues facing our community. We need to be focused on job growth, commercial growth, and diminishing train noise. That's a place where we've made strides. Yet, the soccer issue has taken the forefront. It's all anybody wants to talk about."

"And that case goes away with Sheila Henderson dead," Tanner said.

"If only it were that easy." Leed reached up and loosened his tie. "However, we think we may have a solution. We're planning on announcing it at tonight's council meeting."

"Can we get a preview?" Angela asked.

Leed hesitated. Tanner opened his mouth to speak, but Angela silenced him with a hand gesture. The silence stretched uncomfortably in the small conference room, until finally Leed broke.

"Dick's Sporting Good Park has agreed to open up its soccer fields on a limited basis for practices and games. We believe if we combine the programs in the district, require tryouts, and cut members to form the teams that we'll be able to field at least two high school teams eligible to participate in state competitions."

"That's a creative solution," Angela said. "Did you come up with that?"

Leed preened. "I facilitated the discussions and approached Dick's with the idea."

"In other words, no," Tanner said.

The mayor pulled a handkerchief from his pocket and mopped his brow. "It was actually Ken Martinez's idea."

It seemed that rather than expend his energy on seeking revenge, Martinez had sought and found a solution to the problem for Ken Jr. It spoke well of his character, thought Angela, but it didn't explain why he lied about seeing Sheila Henderson the night before she was found dead.

"What about the second lawsuit, Mayor Leed? The one that names you as a defendant," Angela asked.

Again the silence stretched. The room was getting stuffy, and Angela wished Leed would crack the door or offer them some water. On the other hand, she didn't want the spirit of cooperation driven by Leed's obvious discomfort broken. She pressed. "Do you know what's going to happen with the second lawsuit?"

"I'm hoping the matter will be dropped."

Parker had just told them that the lawsuit would be going forward on Leroy Henderson's behalf. Mayor Leed must not have gotten the word.

"Better luck next time," Tanner said.

Leed wiped the politician's smile off his face and looked from Tanner to Angela. She smiled sympathetically.

"We just came from Sam Parker's office," she said. "It doesn't look like anything's changed."

The Mayor looked stunned. Like a puffer fish out of water, his mouth gaped open and then closed. His face deepened to a dark red color.

"Damn!" he said, slamming a fist down on the table. "That bitch has caused me more trouble. Even from the grave, she makes my life difficult."

A lament that killing her hadn't worked, or simply an acknowledgement that the problems he hoped would be resolved because of her death had just resurfaced?

Looking up, the mayor seemed to realize the effect of his outburst. His pudgy hands fluttered the air in front of him. "I apologize for my emotions. It's just that there are much more important things to be addressed in Commerce City and much better ways to spend taxpayers' money than defending ourselves against a frivolous lawsuit brought on by a woman who seemed to thrive on discord and attention."

"Things like 'train noise'?" Tanner asked.

"You mock, but it was listed as the number three concern of our citizens last year. We believe we've solved that problem by creating quiet zones." Leed was back in full politician mode. "On the 96th street crossing we installed an Automated Horn System, the first of its kind in Colorado. It's a device, mounted on a pole at the crossings rather than on the locomotive, that cuts the noise pollution in our neighborhoods for more than 1.5 miles along the tracks at a minimal cost of eight million dollars."

"You said the other concerns were jobs and commercial developments," Angela said.

"That's right. Gang activity is something that's big on our radar. Like the shootings the other night. Those young men were both thought to be gang members, and the shootings appear to be tied to some sort of outside criminal activity."

Right! Possible violations of the Bald Eagle Protection Act of 1940 and the Lacey Act.

"Are there any other council members who feel as passionately as you about Sheila Henderson's lawsuits, Mayor?" Angela asked.

"All of us feel strongly. I think we have a settlement on the soccer problem, but if her suit on the property goes forward and we're forced to pay a settlement for something that happened back in the 1940s, well let's just say it would significantly impact our budget. It would make it nearly impossible for us to implement any of the things we have slated for the upcoming year." He threw his hands up. "Giving her the land is not an option. No, it's our position that if anyone has to pay recompense, it's the U.S. Army. They were the ones who mishandled this by not making payment and not filing the right documents to begin with."

The position made sense to Angela, but then she didn't know the specifics of the case. The outcome seemed destined to end with the court.

"You want to know what I think," Tanner said. "Either way it goes, it's the taxpayers who are getting screwed."

"A very astute observation, Deputy." Leed flashed his politician's smile, apparently regaining his equilibrium. "Now, have I answered all of your questions? I have a council meeting to chair."

"Just one more thing," Angela said. "Where were you two nights ago between the hours of midnight and 8:00 a.m.?"

Leed knitted his eyebrows in surprise. "Home."

"Can anyone verify that?" Tanner asked.

The mayor looked uncomfortable and tugged as his tie again. "No, actually. You see, I live alone. My wife and I are separated. One of the hazards of being a public servant, I'm afraid. She didn't like the hours."

Chapter 15

Angela reported to work the next morning and brought Wayne up to speed on the investigation. After filing paperwork for the DOI, she worked on the backlog of receipts and requests that had come into the repository in the last three days. On average, the repository received six shipments a day of either whole birds or parts and fielded eleven requests for birds or parts from across the United States. There was nearly double the demand than there was supply, and each receipt of an eagle or part required an investigation to ensure no illegal activity had taken place in the act of acquiring.

At noon she ducked out and grabbed lunch, then headed for the Adams County Sheriff's Office. Pushing through the front door, she found the common area of the squad room practically empty. Deputy Tanner sat alone at his station, typing up reports.

Sitting in an adjoining desk chair, she wheeled herself over beside his desk. "Did you have a chance to follow up with Ken Martinez?"

"Yep." Tanner kept typing.

"What did he have to say?"

"He claimed that he bumped into the victim in electronics. Henderson came in and when she saw him she went on the defensive. They exchanged a few words and then he told her that she didn't need to worry about it anymore. He explained that the city council had found a solution."

"So he was aware of the mayor's negotiations?"

"Apparently."

"Did he say why he didn't tell us he had run into Sheila?"

Tanner stopped tapping on the keys and looked up. "He said he thought it would make us more suspicious, given his previous threats."

"He was right."

"Yeah, but from what I can see, it looks like he's in the clear." Tanner went back to typing. "Martinez never left the building or grounds. Not until the next morning."

Angela settled back in the chair. "One down."

Tanner tapped two more keys, then clicked the mouse and sat back in his chair. "Done."

"What about Mayor Leed?"

"I canvased his neighbors. One woman who lives across the street says she saw him come in around dusk and that his car was parked in his driveway all night."

"How can she be sure?" Angela asked. "She couldn't have had eyes on it the whole time."

"She has a dog that she regularly walks. The last time she went out was just before heading to bed at 2:00 a.m. According to her, Leed's car was still parked in the same spot."

"That doesn't mean he didn't go out," Angela said. But it did mean that he wasn't looking good for committing the crime. Without additional evidence or something that pointed directly to him, they were down to the husband, the mystery woman and Sykes's vic, Patrick Begay.

"Let's look at the surveillance tapes from Garcia's," Angela said. "Where's Detective Sykes?"

"The shooting victim came to this morning and he headed to the hospital."

Angela felt a surge of excitement. "Is the guy talking?"

"Sykes didn't say, just that the victim had opened his eyes." Tanner leaned back over his computer. "As for the surveillance tapes, I should be able to pull them up on my computer provided Sykes logged them in correctly." He tapped a few keys. "Yep, here they are."

Angela felt torn between looking at the tapes and heading directly to the hospital to talk with Patrick Begay, but it made sense to check out the tapes first. She pulled her chair in close beside Tanner and leaned neck-and-neck toward the monitor. "Can you pick it up around 8:30 p.m.?"

"Why so early?" Tanner asked, queuing up the film.

"That's when Sykes said the two shooting victims met in the parking lot. I want to see if there's anything, or anyone, who appears suspicious on the tape."

Grainy black-and-white images scurried across the monitor. At around 9:00 p.m., Donny Smith pulled into the parking lot, parked, and idled. Patrick Begay arrived shortly afterwards, parked, locked up his vehicle, and then climbed into Smith's car. The two drove out of the parking lot. Just like Sykes had told them.

"Now fast-forward to 1:00 a.m.," Angela said. "That's about the time Ron Henderson left the bar to have a smoke."

As Tanner closed in on the time, he slowed the playback. Angela watched the images move on the screen. Still in faster motion than normal, the patrons in the parking lot moved around like swift moving mannequins.

"Wait," she said, pointing at the screen. "There."

Tanner backed up the footage and hit play.

At 1:05 a.m., Ron Henderson exited the bar, pulled a cigarette out of a pack he kept in his shirt pocket, and fished a lighter from his pants pocket.

Angela scanned the cars in the parking lot. Near the back, in the dark shadows cast by the trees, she spotted Sheila's 4Runner.

"There." Angela pointed. "Her car is in the right hand corner. Can you tell if she's inside the vehicle?"

Tanner zoomed in on the spot. Sheila was sitting in the driver's seat. Holding up a camera and snapping photos.

Ron seemed to notice her about the same time Angela had. Dropping his cigarette, he ground it out on the sidewalk and went back inside. Sheila got out of her vehicle, crossed the parking lot, and walked around the side of Garcia's to the back.

Had she figured out that Ron had seen her? She must have assumed he would try and escape out the back.

"Pull up the alley-cam."

Tanner scrolled through a list of the video files. "I don't see one."

You're kidding? There has to be an angle that shows the back entrance?"

"Not one that's here."

Damn. "Could it have been erased?"

"Or never collected. Or maybe Sykes just omitted it, because..."

"Because what?"

"Because he can."

Angela let that one sit. She didn't want to believe he was that petty. Unless, maybe he thought she was onto something. "Okay, well at least we know where she went after Walmart. Martinez told you she was in the electronics section, right? Did he tell you what she bought?"

"A camera."

"Tell me someone has that camera. Did they find it inside her car?"

Taylor rummaged on his desk and came up with two copies of the preliminary report from the CSI processing unit. "It came in just before you got here."

The two of them skimmed the report.

No camera. The only items cataloged in addition to the typical contents of a glove compartment were a box of tissues, a pair of binoculars, a spotting scope, and an umbrella. The only prints they had found belonged to either her or her son.

"Guess we need to talk to her husband again," Tanner said. "She probably took the camera home."

"Unless it was stolen or she lost it or hid it or gave it to someone else for safekeeping," Angela said. Two possibilities jumped to mind—her attorney, Sam Parker, or her BFF, Patty Litchfield. "We know she was taking pictures of Ron and that she walked around back of Garcia's. What if she saw Ron's friend exiting and recognized her? Maybe the girlfriend hit her with something and took the camera."

"It makes sense to me," Tanner said. "Or Sheila could have gone home and confronted Ron with her evidence. They could have fought over the camera."

"We don't want to overlook the other possibility. That she had it with her in the Refuge and took pictures of something or someone, pictures that got her killed." Angela pushed to her feet.

"I say we go with a sure thing," Tanner said. "We know she bought a camera before going to Garcia's, and we have video of her using it there. If she confronted Ron's girlfriend and the girlfriend took it, she might have ditched it in back of the bar. There's a dumpster in back. I say we start there."

"I agree," Angela said. "It's worth taking a look."

Chapter 16

Dumpster-diving moved to the top of the list. It was possible that the trash had already been picked up. If not, time was of the essence.

The search proved futile. Tanner had climbed into the eight-foot roll-off, rummaged around, and come up empty handed. In his words, it was an "epic fail."

Their next stop was the Henderson's. So far Ron hadn't lawyered up where it pertained to his wife's death, so they were free to try and talk with him. No one was home.

Back in the patrol car, Tanner turned on the air-conditioning. The temperature outside had climbed to over ninety, and the wet rings in his armpits had expanded until they were visible. Angela wondered if she suffered the same fate, but opted not to look.

"We could head out to the Refuge and see if we can find the camera out there," suggested Angela.

"And scour all fifteen acres? It could be anywhere." Tanner narrowed his eyes at her. "What makes you so hot on proving there's a link between the two murders, anyway? The only thing you have linking the two cases is the random feather you found near the eyrie."

Not you, too. "A feather that just happens to match the feathers found in the back of Smith's car. That places both Sheila and Sykes's shooting victims at the First Creek site close to the same time."

"It could be just a coincidence."

"That's been pointed out, but I don't believe it." Angela knew how lame that sounded. She had nothing to back it up with but the niggling voice in her head that insisted she was on the right track. "We need to check the evidence log for Smith's car. Maybe Sykes found a camera and he's just not telling us."

"First you practically accuse him of hiding surveillance video, now evidence? Why do you think he would sabotage your case?"

"Chalk it up to an old rivalry. Can you check the log?"

Tanner hesitated a moment, then shifted the patrol car into drive, and pulled away from the curb. "Consider it done. But first, how about we go try and talk to Patrick Begay?"

Denver Health Medical Center, located on Bannock Street, held a longtime reputation for being one of the best trauma hospitals in the country. Founded in 1860, one of its first patients had been a doctor, who had been badly injured in a duel. The violent nature of the injury and the doctor's subsequent care had cemented Denver Health's reputation as the "best place in Colorado to be treated for a gunshot wound."

Angela figured it also helped that, for most of the next one hundred fifty years, all of the hard trauma cases had been delivered to their emergency bays. Practice makes perfect.

The jail lockdown unit was located on the bottom floor of the new Western Addition. Angela wasn't impressed. The state of the art facility had all the bells and whistles, but the unit was still in the basement. Artificial light gleamed off of white-tile floors and drab beige walls.

At the guard station at the end of a hallway that led to a set of closed double doors, Angela flashed her credentials.

"We're here to see Patrick Begay," she said to the officer on duty.

The officer took her badge and studied it, then handed her a clipboard. "You'll both need to sign in here. Once I let you through, you'll need to check in with the nurse. Only authorized personnel are allowed in and out, and only two visitors at a time per patient."

Angela scribbled her name and the time on a sign-in sheet and handed the clipboard to Tanner. "Is Detective Sykes still here?"

"I don't know a Detective Sykes, ma'am. Again, check with the nurse. She can tell you."

Tanner handed back the clipboard, then the officer made a phone call.

"You're good to go," he said. Gesturing for them to follow, he led them over to the double doors, swiped a card through the magnetic strip reader on the door, keyed in a four-digit code and let them pass.

Once inside the unit, Angela assessed the layout. The detention area consisted of fourteen rooms positioned in a semi-circle around a central nurses' station. The two rooms closest to the entry door were double occupancy rooms and empty. The other twelve were private rooms, mostly empty. A large white board on the south wall listed bed assignments and patient names. Only six beds were in use. Begay was in room number ten.

The nurse was busy with another patient, so Angela took that as a sign and entered Begay's room. Tanner followed. They stepped up on either side of the bed.

Begay fit the definition of a trauma patient. After the bandage that swaddled his head, the bandages across his chest and abdomen and the PICC line in his chest, the first thing she noticed was that he was handcuffed to the bed. The second thing she noticed was how small he seemed.

"Patrick Begay," she said.

The man in the bed stirred and opened his eyes. "Who are you?"

Angela introduced herself and Deputy Tanner. "We have a few questions about the eagle feathers discovered in your car."

"I don't know nothing."

"Do you know who shot you?" Tanner asked.

"Like I told that other cop, I don't know nothing. And I'm not talking to nobody. I want you to get out." He rattled the handcuff chain against the rail of his bed. "Did you hear me?"

"Calm down, Begay," Angela said. "If you answer our questions, maybe we can help you."

"I don't need your help. I need you to get the hell out of here." Begay rattled his cuffs louder.

"Where did you get the eagle feathers?" Angela asked again.

"I have a right to have them. I am Tsétsêhéstaestse, Cheyenne."

"That doesn't give you the right to take feathers," Angela said.

Begay's face hardened. "Those feathers belong to the church."

"Yeah, what church is that?" Tanner asked.

"The Native American Church." Begay drilled Angela with a defiant stare. "Last I checked we still have a right to religious freedom in this country."

"You're right, but religious freedom doesn't trump federal law. Those feathers were newly harvested, taken without a permit. For a first offense, you're looking at a year in jail and a minimum ten thousand dollar fine. If the judge throws the book at you, you could be facing a two hundred fifty thousand dollar fine."

"Not to mention life in prison for the murder of Sheila Henderson," Tanner said.

Begay whipped his head around, and then winced. "What you talkin' about? We didn't kill nobody. I'm the one who got shot."

"And we're still waiting for you to tell us who shot you," Tanner said.

"I don't know, okay? I didn't see. But I'm not going to lie here and let you pin a murder wrap on me. We didn't hurt nobody."

Angela pulled out a picture of Sheila Henderson. "Have you ever seen this woman?"

Begay squinted at the picture. "Is she dead? She looks dead."

"As a doornail," Tanner said.

Begay pushed the picture away, the handcuff chain clanging against the bed. "I ain't never seen her before. That's the truth." His skin grew paler with each sentence, and Angela wondered if he was lying or if they might be taxing him too much. Suddenly, a nurse appeared in the doorway.

"What are you doing in here?" she demanded, charging into the room. "Mr. Begay is not allowed visitors."

"A detective from our office was just here," Tanner said, "You were busy when we arrived."

"I don't care if I was invisible," the nurse said, herding them into the hall. "All visitors are required to check with the nurses' station before entering any patient's room. What part of before don't you understand?"

Angela felt her cheeks flush.

The nurse put her hands on her hips. "Now, who are you?"

Angela introduced herself and Deputy Tanner. "Begay is a suspect in a federal crime. We needed to ask him a few questions, and I was informed that he had regained consciousness."

"You and that other detective."

Angela figured she was referring to Detective Sykes.

"Like I told him," the nurse continued, holding up three fingers. "Mr. Begay has sustained three gunshot wounds—one to the head, one to the chest, and one to the abdomen. The shot to the chest collapsed one of his lungs and creased the left side of his liver, causing massive internal bleeding. He might be awake, but he doesn't need you badgering him. I suggest you go back to your office and wait until you're officially notified that Mr. Begay is well enough to answer questions. Meanwhile, let me give you the name of his attorney."

Begay had lawyered-up? Angela glanced at Tanner, who shrugged.

The nurse walked over and rummaged around on her desk, then came up with a card and handed it to Angela. On one side, in embossed lettering was the name: Samuel Bernal Parker, Esq.

"That man gets around," Tanner said.

Chapter 17

By the time Angela and Tanner got back to the Adams County Sheriff's Office, Sykes had clocked out for the day. It meant they would have to wait to ask him about whether or not a camera had been found in Smith's car, but it also saved Angela from having to face him again.

She left a note on his desk, and headed home.

Her new place was a two bedroom apartment off of Quebec, and she was still getting used to the change. Struck by the noise of the kids in the pool as she climbed the stairs to the second floor, she longed for the cabin at Boyd Lake. She had loved it up there, stuck in the woods. She missed the solitude.

Waving at the neighbors, who were out on their deck, she let herself in and was bowled over by the air-conditioning. Turning off the central air, she opened the patio slider and slipped back into the heat. Bone-tired after the last four days, she sat down and promptly fell asleep in the deck chair.

Sometime around 1:00 a.m., she'd awakened. Stars twinkled in the sky above her, slightly dimmed by the light pollution of the city. Still, she traced the constellations she remembered—Cassiopeia overhead, The Big Dipper to the north and Pegasus rising. She stayed there until the noise of the cars cruising the city streets drove her inside.

The next morning, she showered, watered her cactus, and headed into the office before 7:00 a.m. She needed to file an update with the Department of Interior.

Leaning back in her chair, she ran through the case to help organize her thoughts. There were several possible suspects, none of them a threat to national security. Ken Martinez was all but ruled out. Mayor Leed's alibi was shaky, but he didn't look good for the murder either. Ellie Parker's alibi was her husband, who appeared to be the attorney-of-record for anyone residing within the city limits. That left Ron Henderson and the mysterious woman who accompanied him to Garcia's at the top of the list.

According to the babysitter, Jessy Martinez, Ron had gone home shortly after being spooked outside the bar. But there was no way of knowing what happened out back of Garcia's between Sheila and the mystery woman, or between Ron and Sheila later that night. As was often the case, it looked more and more like the husband had done it.

Then there were Smith and Begay, and their mysterious accomplice and possible shooter.

Again she found it interesting that in all cases, Sam Parker's name had come up. He represented Ron Henderson in the lawsuits against the city, he represented his wife, and he represented Begay.

Angela booted up her computer and Googled the attorney.

Samuel Bernal Parker was listed as a graduate of the University of Denver, Sturm College of Law. For several years after graduation he worked as a staff attorney at the American Civil Liberties Union of Colorado. He'd opened his own law practice five years ago, and since then had litigated a preponderance of cases involving violations of civil liberties, such as gay equality, criminal justice, immigration rights, government transparency, and freedom of expression and religion.

Honorable causes. And from his own press, it sounded like everyone loved him.

Pulling up public records on his cases, one in particular drew her attention. Several years back, Parker had represented two Native American Church members who had been fired from their jobs for their use of peyote. They had filed claims for unemployment compensation and had been turned down because they had been dismissed from their jobs for "misconduct." Despite the support of a number of religious organizations, reasoning that their right to free exercise of religion should allow their religious use of the drug, the court upheld the denial on the grounds that their job required them to remain drug-free. Ultimately, the case had landed in the U.S. Supreme Court, which upheld the lower court's findings.

Parker had lost.

Her curiosity piqued, Angela conducted a keyword search for "The Native American Church."

Just as Ellie Parker had told her, Sam Parker's reputed ancestor, Quanah Parker, had been central to the founding of the church. While traveling, he had taken the "medicine" for a difficult illness or injury, became a leading advocate of peyote, and was instrumental in turning back laws that would have forbidden its use.

According to the official website of the Native American Church, its philosophy represented a fusion of Christianity with traditional American Indian religions in varying degrees. Peyote was regarded as a sacramental substance with divine powers—a "teacher." Vomiting was seen as a cleansing of the impurities present in the mind and body of the user. The psychoactive qualities were believed to enhance one's thinking and behavior. And, not only did peyote have medicinal effects, it deterred the desire for alcohol. Peyote was considered a cure for alcoholism.

The description of the peyote ceremony was also like Ellie had described it, with one exception—now women were welcomed at the ceremonies. At midevening, church members of all genders gathered around an altar inside a teepee. One man, called the road man, presided over the ceremony. He faced east. The cedar man threw chips on the fire to create a cleansing smoke, and then participants passed around peyote cactus and tea. Going around the circle, traditional songs were sung. At midnight, a water woman passed through and there was a break in the ceremony. Then participants reconvened, more songs were sung, prayers were offered, and sometimes healing ceremonies were conducted. At dawn, the road man sang the Dawn Song, the water woman brought more water, and the ceremony ended.

It sounded to Angela like a reason to get high. But according to their literature, the church had an estimated two hundred fifty-thousand members. Not all of them could be stoners.

"Find out anything interesting?" a voice asked from the doorway. Angela looked up to find Wayne leaning against the doorjamb. She filled him in on what she knew.

"Maybe you need to talk with Sam Parker again," Wayne said.

"And ask him what? He's not going to incriminate either of his clients, or compel either of them to talk."

"Does he represent the husband in the matter of his wife's death?"

"Not that I'm aware of." Which meant, technically she could still talk to Ron Henderson about Sheila's death without going through his attorney. "What I really need is a warrant to search the Henderson house for the camera."

"Can Deputy Tanner arrange for one?"

"I'll ask."

"What about the murder weapon?"

"Undetermined. The coroner ruled out the steering wheel." She supposed they could check the alley in back of Garcia's again.

"Any other leads?"

"Not unless it had something to do with the lawsuit over the land she claims is still hers."

"Sheila Henderson vs. the U.S. Army et al. Forget that," Wayne said. "Focus on the husband. Find that mystery woman of his and you'll have your answers."

So much easier said than done.

Chapter 18

After checking the backlog of work at the National Eagle Repository, Angela opted to ignore Wayne's advice and pulled up what information she could on the Arsenal land Sheila Henderson claimed she still owned.

Homesteaded by Charles M. Eli out of Kansas City, Missouri records showed that Eli, his wife and three offspring had farmed a piece of property in Section 6 and 5, near the mouth of First Creek. Right near the area where Sheila's body had been found.

Angela accessed the historical data on the Arsenal and pulled up an old survey that showed the approximate location. From the markings on the map, it would include part of the eagles' roost and the eagles' nest.

According to an article in the Rocky Mountain News, Eli's great-great-great-grandson and Sheila's great-grandfather was still farming the land in 1942, when he and his family were forcibly removed by the U.S. Army. A more recent article in The Denver Post, digging into the dispute, indicated that no official survey of the property boundaries had ever been done. It also noted that this was the same area where some of the sarin bomblets had been discovered.

Maybe the reason Sheila was so interested in the eagles' roost had nothing to do with the birds and everything to do with denoting the boundaries of her ancestral land. Maybe in the process of exploring the boundaries, she had stumbled upon something she shouldn't.

Making a copy of the survey map, Angela went to find Wayne. He was out, so she scribbled a note and left it on his desk, telling him what she'd discovered and that she was going to go check it out. If Sheila had found something that had gotten her killed, Angela figured at least one person should know where she was headed. She tried calling Tanner from the truck, but the call went straight to voice mail.

So much for backup.

She wondered if that was how Ian had felt the night he had died. She had been dispatched, but arrived too late. Let's hope she didn't meet a similar fate.

Angela parked her truck in the turnaround where they'd seen signs of a scuffle and re-canvased the area. This time she knew exactly what she was looking for—a weapon that might have been used to hit Sheila in the head. Or an eagle carcass, which would explain the eagle feathers found in Begay's possession. Or a camera that may or may not contain incriminating photographs.

Taking a closer look around the area where the fracas had been, Angela found one or two branches pitched aside that could have served as a club. None showed any evidence connecting with a human head— no blood, no latent hairs. She then walked both sides of the stand of trees with the eagles' nest and found nothing.

Studying the map, she located the approximate southern boundary of the Eli acreage and walked it, cutting straight west from the nesting tree and across Chambers. The land here was covered in short grass—blue grama, buffalo grass, and sagewort—and dotted with purple pasture thistle. She jumped First Creek, which here amounted to little more than a ditch with a trickle of water bordered on both sides with slightly greener vegetation. Two hundred feet more, she came to the edge of a small tributary and turned north.

She walked along the edge of the tributary and stopped underneath a small stand of Cottonwoods to scan the fields. The deer droppings on the trail were the only indication anything or anyone had been there.

Continuing north to the split of the creek, she stopped. The western boundary of the Eli homestead fell outside the vegetation growing along the creek. Large Cottonwoods, willows, and a thicket of wild plums mixed with skunkbrush crowded the creek banks, and Angela skirted the tangle on the outside.

This had been a colossal waste of time. Wayne was right. There was nothing here.

No sooner had her thoughts passed when she spotted a trampled area and broken branches leading toward the creek. Squatting, she studied the ground. Several partial boot prints were etched into the dirt. She caught herself smiling. The disturbance was recent. This July, Colorado had seen its share of warm and dry weather; but on the weekend prior to Sheila's murder, a front moving through had brought afternoon rains and windy conditions. The presence of boot prints now meant that whoever had made the prints had been there in the past five days.

It also meant that whoever had visited the creek had done so in violation of posted orders.

It could easily have been kids in search of a secluded place to make out, but Angela's voice told her it had something to do with why Sheila Henderson had ended up dead. Angela snapped a few pictures, then stepped over the footprints and pushed her way through the crush of branches. Once past the tangle, the vegetation through the trees opened up and she slowed her pace, listening for sounds. All was quiet, except for a woodpecker somewhere in the trees above her.

Pushing through another tight section of thicket, she reached a clearing on the edge of the creek. The ground here had been trampled, and in the center were the remnants of a campfire.

Angela's heart banged in her chest, and she looked around to make sure she was alone.

Walking carefully around the outside of the clearing, she surveyed the scene and quickly realized this was not just any camp.

Located on the edge of Denver, the Refuge had its share of squatters—homeless people who were just looking for a place to settle. The new barrier fence and stepped up patrols had mostly put an end to it, but occasionally a ranger would stumble upon a tent and some person or persons bent on living off the land.

This was not one of those cases. It was easy to see where three main poles had been set into the ground for support, and where nine more poles had been added. Someone had erected a teepee in this clearing. And, based on the look of the fire pit, it hadn't been too long ago.

Could Begay and Smith have conducted a Native American Church ceremony here? Begay would have deemed this land as belonging to Tsétsêhéstaestse, the people.

Angela pulled out her phone. The chances of someone stumbling upon the camp would've been slim. If Sheila had come across this, she could well have been in the wrong place at the wrong time. Angela needed some backup.

Hitting speed dial for Wayne, she heard a crackling in the thicket just as the phone rang on the other end. Quickly she disconnected the call and turned the volume off on her phone. Something or someone was pushing toward her through the trees. Logic told her it was a deer headed for the water. Adrenaline suggested it was someone returning to the scene of the campfire.

Sykes's mystery shooter? He was the one person still unaccounted for, and someone capable of murder.

The crackling grew louder and Angela moved into the cottonwoods that bordered the creek. She un-holstered her gun, then using her keypad, she texted a message to Tanner and pushed send.

The sound of a message hitting a phone sounded from the other side of the clearing.

"Come out, come out, wherever you are," Tanner hollered.

Angela stepped out from behind the tree. "I just texted you."

"I know."

Then, Sykes—red-faced and puffing—pushed into the open. "What's this? A reunion?"

"Damn, you two scared me," Angela said moving further into the clearing.

"Yeah? Well, I'd like to know what the hell you're doing out here." Sykes said.

"I could ask you the same thing," Angela said. Technically, she was the one who had every right to be here. They were the ones who were in a closed area of the Refuge. They should have been accompanied.

"Have you touched anything?" Sykes asked.

Angela checked her anger. Now was not the time to spar. "Of course not. I came out here on a hunch and stumbled upon the path. I was just calling for backup when I heard you."

"What kind of hunch?" Tanner asked.

"The kind she's not supposed to be following," Sykes said. "Right, Dimato?"

Her anger flared. "For what it's worth, it had nothing to do with trying to connect the cases."

He grinned. "Of course not."

"I'm telling you the truth." Angela clued them in on her suspicions that Sheila had been out here scouting the homestead boundaries. "It was purely happenstance that I stumbled upon this site. But now that we know it's here, it looks more and more like I may have been right that the two cases are intertwined."

Sykes pulled a handkerchief out of his back pocket and mopped his brow. Looking as sweaty and disheveled as he did, Angela wondered what she'd ever seen in him.

"I went back and talked to Begay again this morning," Sykes said. "He tipped me off to what he and Smith were doing out here. The poor guy was spooked after you showed him the photo of that dead woman."

"Did he admit to seeing her?"

Sykes shoved his handkerchief back in his pocket. "Nope. Before he could elaborate, his attorney showed up and told him to shut his mouth."

"Parker?"

"That's the guy."

"But if Begay wanted to talk..."

"Doesn't matter, Angel. The attorney set the nurse on me, and the bulldog was glad to oblige. They claimed the 'boy' wasn't competent to talk because of all the pain medication, ya da, ya da. 'Boy.'" He made quote signs in the air. "Since when are you still a boy at twenty-seven?"

"How much did he tell you?"

"Before the gag order? He told me that they had held a meeting out here on Indian land. Apparently there were a bunch of them, but he flat out refused to give any names. He claims everyone had cleared out by 6:00 a.m. He and Smith were the last to leave, around 6:45 a.m. They were ambushed ten minutes later, a block short of Garcia's parking lot."

"What about you?" Angela asked Tanner, feeling somewhat betrayed that he was hanging out with Sykes. "Why are you here?"

"Beats riding the desk." He leaned close to her ear. "Actually, Sykes needed backup."

Angela chuckled. "And you drew the short straw? Lucky you."

"Can it," Sykes said, appearing to be all business. "What have you found so far?"

Angela turned her attention back to the clearing. "You can see where the poles of the teepee were jammed into the ground, and the remains of the fire. I took a few pictures. Otherwise, I just got here myself."

"Good. So we'll search by grid," Sykes said. "Angel, you take streamside. I'll walk the middle. Tanner, you take the west side."

There were lots of methods for walking a crime scene, but the grid worked best. First, they would walk parallel in one direction, an arm's length or more apart. Then, after marking anything of interest, they would move forty-five degrees and walk it again.

The three of them studied the ground for anything that seemed out of place—a footprint, a gum wrapper, hair, or fibers—and turned up nothing.

When they finished, Sykes moved to the fire pit. Bending down, he gently pushed several unburned branches to the side. That's when Angela spotted the charred remains. Her stomach pitched and she fought the urge to throw up.

"Is that what I think it is?" Tanner asked.

"It's part of the eagle carcass we've been looking for." From where she stood, she could see fragments of the bird's charred breast plate, with nubs of ribs attached and a partial skull. She doubted they would find any sign of its beak or talons. Angry tears stung her eyes.

"Come over here and take a picture," Tanner said, lifting a portion of the carcass with a stick.

Angela forced herself to move forward and snap a few shots on her phone. Finally, she turned away and walked to the edge of the clearing. "I don't think there's any doubt now about the cases being connected."

"How do you figure, Angel?"

"Are you serious? It's clear that Begay and Smith killed the eagle, harvested the feathers, and then tried to burn the evidence."

"Or somebody else did and used the feathers to set them up."

Angry, she turned on Sykes. "Can we agree on one thing? That the feathers were taken here?"

He looked amused, but nodded.

"And that one of the feathers from this bird is the one Wayne and I found, across First Creek at the turn around on Chambers near the eyrie?"

"Okay, I'll give you that, too."

"We collected tire tracks that day that appear to match Sheila Henderson's car," Angela said. "We're still waiting on the CSI report for official confirmation, but if they are, then—"

"The cases cross paths," Sykes finished.

Tanner was already on the phone asking to speak to someone in the CSI lab. After a short conversation, he grinned and hung up. "We've got a match, and they're sending someone this way."

"The problem is, it still doesn't prove your victim was in possession of the feather," Sykes said. "Or that my guys took it over to First Creek."

Angela tamped down her irritation. How like him to do the two-step when things weren't dovetailing his way. The man was the king of ambiguityalways playing the devil's advocate, never taking a stand on anything, refusing to ever see it anyone else's way. Hadn't he just said it would prove the cases bisected? "Two minutes ago you were willing to concede that there was enough circumstantial evidence to draw a conclusion."

"Yes, that your vic and my vics crossed paths," Sykes said. "But that doesn't prove they ever actually encountered each other. Maybe Smith and Begay killed the eagle at the turn around. Maybe one of its feathers came out. You can't prove Sheila Henderson knew anything about the death of the bird."

Frustrated, Angela turned her back on Sykes. He was shooting holes in her theory faster than she could formulate it. The fact that Wayne or a judge would have done the same thing was of no consolation.

"Look, Angel, it's not a bad scenario, but you have to be able to back it up. Let me take another run at Begay. I have some leverage to question him again now that we have the bird carcass. His attorney could still argue that someone else was involved, but the circumstantial evidence of the bones in the campsite and the feathers in the car will go a long way toward making your felony case in violation of all those

Acts. And, with a little luck, I'll turn up something that helps you solve the Henderson murder."

Angela turned around and stared at Sykes. "Do you really believe you're going to be the one to solve my case?"

"I didn't mean it like that, Angel."

Yes, you did. He had never taken her seriously. Well, she would show him what she was capable of. "Do you believe in coincidence, Sykes?"

He nodded. "You bet. I've seen way too many cases where we thought we had our man and all we had was an unfortunate twist of fate. That's why our justice system demands definitive proof before convicting a man of something as heinous as murder."

It wasn't the answer Angela had expected, but he had made his point. Without solid evidence, she had nothing more than conjecture.

"Yeah, but how often does an innocent man get convicted?" Tanner asked.

Angela knew the answer. "About as often as a guilty man goes free."

Chapter 19

Sykes had left and gone back to the station, leaving Tanner and Angela to wait for CSI.

"What do you think the team is going to find out here?" Tanner asked as they walked up to where her truck was parked. "We walked the grid and found nothing."

"The bones will give us DNA and we can match the feathers to the carcass, including the feather we found at the turnaround. If we're lucky, maybe CSI can pull a hair or something that will help us ID some of the others who were out here that night."

If they got real lucky, maybe they'd get something that tied Sheila Henderson to the scene. Not that Angela harbored any real hope. The CSI solutions that you see on TV were a far cry from what happened in real life. The everyday reality was that most CSI labs were outdated and backlogged. Only the fact that DOI was involved made dragging CSI out here and running the tests feasible.

"So what's next?" Tanner asked, putting down the tailgate on the truck and taking a seat. Angela slid up beside him and dangled her feet.

"I guess we're back to the husband." The latest stats showed that twenty-six percent of all women murdered were killed by their husbands or boyfriends. In this case, there was a cheating husband, and an indication that the wife knew he was cheating."

"What about the girlfriend?" he said.

"It would help if we could identify her."

"No shit, Sherlock."

Angela thought about her last conversation with Wayne. "It would help if we could find the missing camera. Any chance you could arrange for a warrant to search the Henderson house?"

"I'm all over it." He slid off the tailgate, then stopped and turned to look at her. "So what's the deal with you and Sykes?"

Angela felt her face flush.

"Yeah, that's what I'm talkin' about. What happened between you two?"

"Nothing."

"Don't give me that."

"Look, just drop it, okay? It's ancient history."

"You're not that old."

Angela could see he wasn't about to let her off easy. "We spent some time together, that's all. I thought he was a nice guy. It turned out he is an arrogant jerk."

"Doing a little horizontal Mambo?"

"Tanner!"

Two hours later, warrant in hand, they ascended the front steps of the Henderson residence. It was late in the day. The sun was dipping toward the Continental Divide, casting long shadows. The wind had picked up, but the day was still hot and dry.

Leroy Henderson opened the door. "Yeah?"

Angela pushed her sunglasses up on her head. "Is your dad here?"

"No. He's not home yet."

"Is there anyone here besides you?" Tanner asked.

"No."

Angela turned back toward the contingent of police officers headed up the walk and called out, "We need someone from social services before we can enter. There's only a minor child at home."

One of the officers turned back, jogged to his car, and got on the radio.

"What's going on?" Leroy's voice sounded small, and Angela felt badly that she was responsible for causing him stress.

"Deputy Tanner and I have a warrant to search your house," she explained. "We're looking for a camera that your mother had with her the night before she died."

"I haven't seen it. You'll have to ask my dad."

"That's just it, we don't have to ask, kid," Tanner said. "You see this piece of paper? It gives us the right to come inside and look around."

Angela pulled Tanner back from the door and shook her head. "Not with Leroy in the house alone. Without his dad here, we have to have someone come and stay with him while we search."

"You've got to be kidding me? How long is that going to take?" Tanner asked.

It was a legitimate question. The last time they'd called for a child advocate, the person never showed up.

Angela glanced back at Leroy. Tears pooled in his eyes and his look filled her with guilt. "What time does your dad usually get home?"

Leroy shrugged. "It depends on how his day goes."

"Do you think you could get him on the phone?" Angela asked.

Leroy stood firm. "I'm not supposed to bother him at work."

"Even in the case of an emergency?" Angela could see the neighbors coming out on their porches. One woman held up her cell phone, likely taping the interaction. They had to play this one by the book.

Leroy looked uncertain. "Is this an emergency?"

"You bet your—"

Angela put her hand on Tanner's sleeve. "Yes, I think this qualifies."

While Angela and Tanner stood on the front porch, Leroy called his father. She could hear Ron Henderson yelling in the background, and then Leroy shoved the phone into her hand.

"What the hell do you think you're doing?" Henderson screamed when she put the phone up to her ear. "You can't harass my son like this."

"No one has done anything to your son, Mr. Henderson. We've got social services on the way. We will wait until they arrive and Leroy's out of the house before executing the warrant."

"I want to be there."

"You are welcome to come home, but we are under no obligation to wait for you to be present. Once social services is here, we are going inside."

When Angela handed the phone back to Leroy, she heard his dad berating him for opening the door. Then he told him to go back inside and throw the deadbolt. Stepping forward, she put her foot across the threshold.

The door swung closed, bouncing off the toe of her boot.

"I have to lock the door now," Leroy said.

"Don't make this harder on yourself, kid," Tanner said.

It took ten more minutes for a child advocate to arrive. By then, Leroy was in tears, and he flailed around and struggled as they removed him from the house. The neighbor caught it all on tape. No doubt Ron and his attorney would try and use it against them.

Inside, the officers fanned out. The warrant was for a search of the premises to locate a digital camera, like the one seen in Sheila's possession on the night before she was found dead. It allowed for a search of the garage and all vehicles on the premise.

Angela was standing at the front window when Ron Henderson pulled into the driveway. Leroy was sitting at the curb with the child advocate, but Henderson ignored them and bounded up the front steps.

"Show me the f-ing warrant," he demanded. Angela shoved it into his hands. Two minutes later, Sam Parker arrived.

"I want you off my property," Ron shouted.

"Ron, calm down! Let me see the warrant." Parker took it, scanned it quickly, and then looked up at Angela. "You're reaching here."

"Why do you say that, Mr. Parker? We have a camera missing that may have the piece of incriminating evidence we need to prove your client had something to do with the murder of his wife."

Ron blanched. "What? I'm telling you, I didn't kill my wife."

"Then do you want to tell us who you were with that night at the bar?" Angela said. "The night your wife went down to Garcia's with her camera and took your picture?"

"Keep your mouth shut, Ron," Parker said.

Ron turned his head away.

"I didn't think so." Angela cast a look over her shoulder in Leroy's direction. "We'll make this as quick as we can."

Parker turned to Ron. "Do you have any cameras on the premises?"

"What?"

"Do you have any cameras, Ron? If you do, they will find them. They're going to take any camera paraphernalia and all your laptops and computers where you may have stored photos, too. You can make this easier on yourself by just turning them over."

"It's not going to prevent us from searching, Mr. Parker," Angela said.

Tanner appeared in the hallway to the kitchen, holding a camera in the air. "Found one."

The officers searched the entire house, the garage, and Ron's car, but only turned up the one camera. An examination showed the memory card was missing and all pictures had been erased. It was bagged into evidence and carted away. Several items related to the camera were confiscated too, as well as one desktop computer and two laptops. One appeared to be Leroy's.

"I hope you're satisfied," Parker said, once the last computer had been hauled out to one of the patrol cars. "I'm expecting this is the last we're going to see of you."

Angela smiled. "Thank you for your cooperation."

At the front door, she passed Leroy, who dashed inside and headed for his father. Ron cuffed him in the back of the head. "How stupid can you be, boy? Never, never open the door when you're here by yourself."

The action bordered on child abuse, and Angela considered having Ron arrested right then and there. Instead, she cleared her throat and gave him the evil eye.

Ron stared for a moment. Then, looking away, he patted Leroy on the shoulder and directed him toward the kitchen. "We're almost done here, son. Go on and get yourself a snack. I'll be there in a minute."

Better.

Chapter 20

On Monday afternoon, Tanner called.

"We came up empty," he said. "We dissected the computer and laptops. There were no photos taken at the Refuge, except for a few of the eagles in flight. Nothing contained anything incriminating. There were no photographs taken at Garcia's, either. Sorry, Angela. Any other leads to exhaust?"

"Not at the moment."

Hanging up the phone, Angela rubbed her eyes, then propped her elbows on the desk and rested her head in her hands. Unless someone from the bar came forward to identify their mystery woman or Begay coughed up names in a plea bargain for a reduced sentence, she had nothing more to go on. They'd run down every lead and turned over every rock.

"Giving up?" Wayne said from the doorway.

Angela straightened. "Regrouping."

"Yeah? Because you look a little despondent there."

"I feel like I'm missing something."

"It happens. I've got one piece of good news for you. The DOI is satisfied that we're looking at nothing more than a tragic death on public lands with this one. Unless something new comes up, we're done filing reports."

A silver lining. "That's great." Then she had a sudden moment of trepidation. "You aren't suggesting we let this case go, are you?"

Angela wasn't ready to call it quits. She had promised Leroy the morning they'd found his mother in that field that she would figure out what had happened. She intended to keep her promise. Besides, there was no way she wanted to turn this case over to someone like Sykes.

Wayne shook his head. "Not unless it interferes with keeping up on the workload."

Angela took his warning to heart and immersed herself in the backlog of repository work for the rest of the day. Knocking off just after 5:00, she decided to pay Patty Litchfield a visit on the way home. She'd been on Angela's mind most of the day. Patty was Sheila's best friend and the one person she might have trusted. It stood to reason, if Sheila had something to hide—like a camera or the memory card from a camera—that's who she would turned to.

Patty opened the door on the third knock.

"Oh, it's you." She looked outside. "Do you have a warrant to search my house, too?"

"I just want to talk."

Patty looked her up and down, and then shrugged. "It's a small neighborhood. Word gets around."

"Do you mind if I come in?"

Patty shrugged again. "What the heck? We can go out back."

Angela followed her through the house to the patio off the kitchen.

"You know, Leroy was pretty badly shaken up after your search and seizure yesterday. I went over there after you left. He had locked himself in his room and he refused to come out. Ron had to nearly bust the door down to get him to eat dinner."

Even though there had been little choice, Angela felt a pang of guilt. "Is he okay now?"

"I don't know. I didn't stay long. I just wanted Ron to know that I have his back, just like I had Sheila's."

"Even if Ron's the one who hurt her?" Angela asked, bracing for the reaction.

Patty reared up in her chair. "He would never do that. Even with all their problems, he cared for her. She was the mother of his kid."

"Is that why he was having an affair?"

Patty looked away. "That's just what Sheila thought. She wasn't sure."

Angela sat back in her seat. "It turns out she was right."

That got Patty's attention. She stared at Angela. "Is it Ellie?"

"You see, that's the thing. Ellie Parker was there, but she left early. We can prove that. Still, we know he was there with someone until the

early hours of the morning." Angela told Patty how they had learned
that Sheila had cased out Garcia's the night before her body was found.
"That's why we searched the Henderson's house. We needed to find
that camera."

"Did you?"

"No, but then I got to thinking. If I was a woman who had just
snapped pictures of my husband's mistress, what would I do with
them?" Angela waited to see if Patty would fill in the gap and admit to
having the memory card.

"And?" Patty asked.

"I thought she might have brought them to you. For safekeeping."

Patty looked surprised. "No. She didn't bring anything here. I went
to bed early that night. The next morning, she was dead."

"Any chance she could have left it here without your knowledge? Did
she have a key to your house?"

"Of course." Patty smoothed the front of her capris. "But if she'd
come inside, the alarm would have chirped. I'm a very light sleeper."

"What about someone else? A minister, or another friend."

Patty made a face, and tipped her head to the side like she was
thinking, then shook her head. "I can't think of anyone. She wasn't
religious, and I don't know who else she would trust. I was the only one
she'd told about her suspicions." Patty took a deep breath, and then
suddenly stood. "All of this is just so upsetting. I could use a drink. Do
you want one?"

"No, thanks, I shouldn't," Angela said. Technically she was off-duty,
but she was still driving the USFW truck.

"Oh, come on," Patty said through the screen door to the kitchen.
"One drink won't hurt you, and I hate to drink alone."

"Maybe some lemonade or iced tea."

"Lemonade. You got it. Rum?"

"No, thank you."

"Ice?"

"Sure."

It only took Patty a few minutes to come back outside with two drinks
in hand. She handed Angela a tall glass filled with ice and lemonade,

and then took a long sip out of her glass. "Oh, that tastes good. There's nothing quite like a gin and coke."

Angela set her glass down on the patio table harder than she had intended. Patty jumped. How had she missed it? "It's you."

"What are you talking about?" Patty said, setting down her own glass and blotting the front of her blouse with a napkin. "Look what you made me do."

"You are the one having an affair with Sheila's husband."

Patty's face drained of color. "That's ludicrous. She was my best friend."

"The bartender at Garcia's couldn't remember your face, but he never forgets a drink. Nobody drinks gin and coke without ice. Except you."

Patty dropped her napkin and her face crumpled. "You have to believe me, I didn't mean for it to happen."

That's what they all say. "How did it start?"

"You have to understand, Sheila wasn't easy to live with. Ron needed someone to talk to. He would come by here sometimes and ask me what I thought about the things she would do. One day, he just leaned over and kissed me."

Angela didn't care about her justifications, just the details about the night Shelia was murdered. "What happened that night at Garcia's?"

"Ron and I had never gone out before. Garcia's is sort of a dive bar. Sometimes he goes there with the guys after work, but just because it's close." Patty picked up the napkin and started pulling at it with her fingers. "No matter what you might think, Ron and I were in love. We wanted to be together. We just didn't know how we were going to tell Sheila and Leroy. We were trying to figure it out."

"I take it he called you from the bar," Angela said.

"After everyone left. Sheila was supposed to be home with Leroy. No one from our neighborhood would ever go there. All we wanted was just to go out and have some fun for a change. Have people see how happy we were together instead of sneaking around all the time, you know?"

"I'm listening."

"We were having a great time, and then Ron went out front for a cigarette. When he came back, he was all upset. He said Sheila was outside, and that she had a camera. He told me to go out the back, while he went out to confront her."

So far, her story matched the bartender's. "What happened next?"

Patty reached over, picked up her glass and took a huge swallow of gin and coke. "Sheila was waiting for me in the alley."

Angela waited for her to continue, but Patty just stared into her glass. "And?"

Patty glanced up. "She looked so hurt. I told her how sorry I was, and that it didn't change the fact I loved her. She and I were best friends since grade school. I told her that sometimes friends just fall in love with the same man. That she'd had her time with Ron, and that now it was my time."

Angela couldn't help but laugh. "I bet that went over well."

"She told me she never wanted to talk to me again."

Angela leaned toward Patty. "Did she say she was going to confront Ron?"

"No. She just walked away. That was the last time I saw her." Patty took another slug of her drink. "The worst part is, now Ron says we shouldn't be together. He's worried about what people will say if they find out. He says he feels too guilty. Well, he wasn't worried when he was sneaking in my backdoor."

"What did you do after Sheila left?" Angela asked.

"I came home and waited for Ron to call. He never did."

"I'm going to ask again. Do you know if Sheila went home and confronted him?" If so, there might have been a confrontation. He was a man prone to violence. Angela'd seen him whack his son in the back of the head.

"I don't know," Patty said. "But if Ron said she was home in the morning, she was home."

Angela admired the loyalty, but unlike eagles that mate for life, humans were a fickle lot. "You're better off without him."

Chapter 21

The minute Angela hit the truck she called Tanner and told him about her conversation with Patty Litchfield.

"Maybe she helped him kill her?"

"I don't think so." Angela didn't get the feeling that Patty was of much danger to anyone but herself. The problem was that she wasn't sure if Ron had killed Sheila either. He was like most bullies. Easy to back down, if you were brave enough to stand up to them.

"What are you thinking?" Tanner asked.

"I say let's bring him in for questioning, and hope we get to him before Patty lets him know they're blown."

Henderson walked into the Sheriff's office at 10 a.m. the next morning with his attorney Sam Parker leading the way. Angela watched in dismay as they were shown into the conference room.

"I hoped to do this in interrogation," she said to Tanner as they walked down the hall.

"Parker talked to the D.A."

The two men were seated at a large table drinking coffee. Parker stood when Angela entered the room.

"Agent Dimato." He nodded. "Deputy."

"Sit," she said. "Mr. Henderson, we just have a few questions for you."

"Let's get to it," Parker said.

"We asked you earlier who you were with at Garcia's the night before your wife was discovered dead. I'm going to ask you again."

Henderson remained stone-faced, while Parker leaned in. "I don't see the relevance. That was hours before my client's wife died."

"Ever hear of 'talk and die' syndrome?" Tanner asked.

Both men and Angela turned to Tanner. He must have been doing some research.

"Do tell," Parker said.

"It's when someone is struck in the head and suffers a brain bleed. Sometimes a victim can go hours before showing any symptoms."

"Mr. Henderson," Angela said, recapturing his attention. "We know that your wife had a confrontation with your mistress in the alley behind Garcia's the night before her body was discovered."

"Are you suggesting my client's mistress murdered his wife?"

"No, we're suggesting that Sheila went home that night and confronted your client, who then struck her, just like he struck his son last Friday, causing the fatal injury." Angela watched to see the effect her words were having on Henderson. At the mention of him striking his son, his face turned red and he moved to the edge of his seat.

"I didn't kill my wife," he said.

"Let me do the talking, Ron," Parker said.

"No, because I have nothing to hide. I didn't do anything wrong."

"You lied to us," Tanner said.

"I didn't want to drag Patty's name into this."

"Patty Litchfield," Angela said, just to get confirmation from him.

"I know you figured it out. I'm not proud of myself."

"What did you hit her with, Henderson?" Tanner asked.

"I didn't—"

"Be quiet, Ron." Parker interjected. "They're fishing." The attorney repositioned himself in his chair, gathering up the papers in front of him. "Do you have a murder weapon?"

Tanner looked at Angela.

"I would like Mr. Henderson to tell me what happened that night."

"And he's told you," Parker said. "He didn't talk to her."

"Mr. Parker, your client has been lying to us all along," Angela said. "First he's not having an affair, but later, when confronted with eyewitness accounts, he admits he was in the bar with someone. He won't say who, but then he admits to banging his wife's best friend. He denies knowing about a camera that's clearly visible on the surveillance videos, and then we find what we believe is the camera, in his house, with the memory card removed."

"We're done here." Parker picked up his papers. "Unless you intend to charge my client, we're leaving."

Angela knew she couldn't stop them. The case they had compiled against Ron was circumstantial at best. There was nothing substantial to back up any of their allegations—no witnesses, no murder weapon, no proof.

"Let's go, Ron," Parker said.

"Wait a minute," Henderson said. "I want to say something."

"Ron." Parker's tone clearly held a warning.

"No, they accused me of hitting my wife, but I read the coroner's report. It said there was a distinct pattern to the bruising on her head."

"Ron!" Parker's voice commanded silence.

Ron stabbed a finger toward Angela. "You searched my house and you didn't find anything."

"We didn't have a warrant to search for a weapon, just the camera."

"But if you'd found a weapon, you would have confiscated it and arrested me."

"That's enough, Ron." Parker grabbed his client by the elbow and pushed him toward the door. "Don't say another word."

"You leave me and my son alone."

Angela and Tanner stood in the hall and watched them walk away. Ron yanked his arm free of Parker's grip and stormed ahead of him out the doors.

"Another epic fail," Tanner said.

"Not necessarily," Angela said, turning toward Tanner's desk. "Where is the coroner's report?"

Tanner rifled through the papers on his desk, finally coming up with a sheaf of papers. "What are we looking for?"

Angela took the packet and flipped to the appendix with the pictures the coroner had taken of Sheila. One in particular showed her head shaved on one side. A zoomed in photograph displayed a bruise with a distinctive patterning.

"The coroner said that the bruise might have been caused by a stick. Does this look like it was caused by the random marks on a tree branch?"

"Maybe," Tanner said.

"Look closer." Angela pointed out several distinct marks that were mirrored top and bottom. "That isn't a random pattern. It's symmetrical. This pattern's been etched into something. We're barking up the wrong tree. I was right all along."

"What are you talking about?"

"These markings were made by patterns carved into wood."

Angela's excitement grew as she realized what she was seeing and explained her theory to Tanner. "Don't you see? Begay and Smith were conducting a peyote ceremony on the edge of First Creek."

"We're back to the Indians."

"Bear with me. Every member would have had a peyote box, and every peyote box have a stick and a rattle marked with unique, but similar bas-relief carvings."

Tanner was quick on the uptake. "Markings that might match the bruises on Sheila Henderson's head."

"You got it." Angela smiled. This time, she felt sure they were onto something. "Begay's and Smith's peyote boxes have to be in the evidence locker."

It took them under ten minutes to check. Both boxes had been logged in, and both were intact. Tanner and Angela checked the carvings on the sticks and rattles. Neither matched the marks on Sheila's head. But either one could have used someone else's stick from that night.

"We need to talk to Sykes," Angela said. "He was going to talk to Begay."

Sykes wasn't in the office. Tanner tried reaching him, but his cell phone defaulted to voice mail.

So much for being on duty 24/7.

"I'll try on my way back to my office," she said. "Meanwhile, if he shows up, keep him cornered."

Pulling into the refuge, Angela tried him again. This time Sykes answered on the fourth ring.

"I clocked out for lunch. A man's entitled."

"I want to know what Begay told you about the night Sheila was murdered."

"He didn't tell me anything. He admitted he and Smith conducted a peyote ceremony out in the woods, but he wouldn't name anyone else present. You've got nothing to go on, Angel. Give it up."

Angela clicked off taking some satisfaction in the knowledge she at least had a lead he didn't know about, even if it was a lead she couldn't follow up on. She could try and talk to Begay herself, to see if he would give up his cohorts. But, she would have to go through Sam Parker again. He was Begay's attorney-of-record. She could try contacting the Native American Church. It wasn't likely they'd have records on any unsanctioned peyote ceremonies, but she might be able to obtain a list of members in the area. Again, she'd have to go through Parker.

Talk about coincidence.

Or was it?

Angela skootched up straighter behind the wheel. Sam Parker claimed to be a descendant of the founding father of the Native American Church, Quanah Parker. He owned a peyote box. What if he had been the one Sheila has spotted on the Refuge that morning? If even a suggestion of his involvement in something like the peyote ceremony or theft of the eagle feathers leaked out, his reputation would be ruined. Parker banked on his reputation.

Motive and means.

Angela could picture his box sitting on the floor of his living room. She would need another look inside, and some luck it was still intact. Parker was arrogant, but enough to believe he could get away with murder? If she'd been in his shoes, she would have ditched the box, or at least some of its contents. Of course, he also took pride in his heritage. It would mean too much to him to dismantle it completely.

So how could she get her hands on the box? There was no way Parker would let her catalog the contents now, and he'd made it abundantly clear she was to have no more contact with his wife—not without going through him.

Then something Ellie had told Angela niggled in the back of her mind. Ellie had said that Parker was interested in his heritage, but that he didn't have time to invest in it.

Was it possible he'd overlooked the law? To legally possess an eagle feather, he had to be a registered member of the Comanche tribe. If his paperwork wasn't in order, Angela had him.

Parking the truck, she bounded up the stairs to her office and clicked on the computer. Then, pulling up the databases she had for the Comanche tribe, she searched for Samuel Parker's name. Samuel Bernal Parker.

The search came up empty. There was no listing.

To be on the safe side, she then telephoned the Comanche Nation Enrollment Department and spoke to the director. The woman had put her on hold and came back insisting that no one of that name was a registered tribal member. As far as the Comanche were concerned, Samuel Bernal Parker was not Numinu, one of the people.

"Wayne!" Angela sprinted down the hall to her boss's office and found him nose to screen with his computer.

"You're interrupting something."

"It's important." While Wayne might not be as enthusiastic about her plan, Angela needed his help. Before she could enter the Parker residence, she would need to obtain a search and seizure warrant and issue Parker a citation for illegal possession of eagle parts.

While she explained what she needed, she watched Wayne from the opposite side of his large wooden desk. His facial expressions shifted between horrified and mild amusement. "You're serious?"

"Dead serious. We have every right to confiscate the peyote box. Then, once it's in our possession, we can check it against the bruising. Whether or not it's a match, we have him dead to rights on illegal possession of eagle parts."

Wayne pinched his chin between his thumb and fingers. "What level of fine are you thinking?"

"Let's get his attention. How about we hit him with a five thousand dollar fine and one year imprisonment?"

Wayne shook his head. "That will never stick."

"No, but it's a good place to negotiate from."

"I don't know a single judge who will want to issue a search and seizure warrant against Sam Parker."

"He may be a powerful man, but there's got to be somebody out there who doesn't like him."

It took three hours, but they'd finally found someone who wasn't afraid of Sam Parker. By then, Tanner was out on another call, so Angela went without him. A half hour later, parked outside the Parker's residence, Angela radioed the USFW agents in the van behind her.

"Ready?"

"On your 'go,'" said the driver.

The three of them climbed out of their vehicles. With warrants in hand, Angela led the way up the steps and knocked on the front door. Ellie Parker answered, wearing an apron and holding a spatula. She looked surprised to see them.

"You aren't supposed to be here," she said.

"Is Mr. Parker home," Angela asked.

"Of course not, he's still at work."

Angela held out the documents. "I have a warrant for the peyote box, along with a citation for violation of the Bald and Golden Eagle Protection Act."

Ellie took and studied the papers. "This is ridiculous. My husband is a descendant of Quanah Parker. He has a right to those artifacts."

"Not according to law," Angela said, pushing past her into the house. "In order to be legal, he must be a registered member of an Indian tribe. According to the Comanche tribal records, he isn't."

Ellie followed her into the living room. "You have no right to enter my house."

"That paper you're holding gives me the right." Angela spotted the peyote box sitting on the floor near the bookcase.

"You get out of here." Ellie said, brandishing her spatula.

"If you move one step closer, I will hit you with an obstruction charge," Angela said. "And if you touch me with that or get any food on my uniform, I'll charge you with resisting arrest and assaulting a federal officer."

Ellie backed off. While she made a call to her husband, Angela opened the peyote box to make sure all the contents were there.

"Sam? Sam, you need to come home."

Angela closed the box and fastened the clasp. "It looks like everything's here," she said, handing it to one of the USFW officers. "Be careful. It's old."

Ellie moved to block them from leaving. "You can't take that."

"We can," Angela said. "Now, I need you to sign here that you were served with the citation."

"I won't."

"Mrs. Parker, you need to understand something. If you don't sign and get out of our way, I can arrest you for unlawful interference in the execution of a warrant."

"The contents of the box are fragile," Ellie said. "I'll hold you responsible if anything is damaged."

"Maybe we need to make a note then, that there are already two feathers broken on the peyote rattle," Angela said, scribbling that down on the evidence receipt before extending the paper and a pen.

Ellie stared at Angela before taking the receipt. Her hand shook as she initialed the papers. "Sam will be here any minute. If you just wait, he'll be able to clear this entire mess up."

"Not this time," Angela said.

Chapter 22

Wayne was waiting for Angela when she got back to the repository.

"Sam Parker called," he said.

"My guess is he wasn't happy." She showed the officers where to put the box.

"He's threatening to file a lawsuit. Claims we're harassing him because of his representation of our chief suspect."

"Did you tell him our suspect had changed?"

"Absolutely not."

After the officers left to clock out, Angela retrieved the coroner's report and opened the box for Wayne. "Here we go."

She put on a latex glove before reaching inside. Her prints were already on some of the items, and if the peyote box had been recently used—as she suspected it had—she worried too many people would have handled the items to make prints of any value. Still, there was always a chance.

"We'll need CSI to verify any findings," Wayne said.

"Right, but we can do some preliminary findings." Angela flipped the packet open to the close-up of the bruise mark on Sheila Henderson's head. Picking up the rattle, she pointed to the markings on the handle and gourd. "Buffalo tracks."

Holding the rattle near the picture, the two of them studied the markings.

"What do you think?" she asked Wayne, her excitement growing. To her it looked like a match. The bas-relief was thin in areas, and the marks weren't totally clear, but they appeared to be the same size, the same shape as the markings in the picture. "I think we found the murder weapon."

The next day, Angela called Tanner and asked him to meet her at the CSI lab.

"Wayne insists on confirmation, but I think we got him," Angela said, after telling him about the raid on the Parkers.

Unfortunately, the CSI couldn't substantiate. "I can't be sure. There are a lot of similarities. I can say there's a likelihood of a match, but I think you'll need some other forensic evidence to make it stick."

"What about fingerprints on the handle?" Angela felt desperate.

"It came up clean."

He'd been smart enough to wipe off his prints. All prints.

"So we're back to nothing," Angela said, walking back to the squad room with Tanner.

"Not exactly. If he's convicted on illegal possession of eagle feathers, he could go to jail. He'll for sure pay a hefty fine."

"That's a far cry from first degree murder charges. Frankly, I doubt he'll get much more than a slap on the hand. In cases like these, judges tend to be lenient with first offenders, especially ones with Sam Parker's clout and alleged pedigree."

"Begay doesn't know that," said a voice to their left. Angela turned to find Sykes partially hidden behind the computer screen at his desk. He didn't look up.

"Except we can't talk to him, remember?" she said.

"That's all changed."

Angela stopped walking. "How so?"

Sykes looked up and smiled at her over the top of his monitor. "I got notice this morning. Parker removed himself as Begay's attorney."

Angela figured it had something to do with his being outed for not being on the Comanche Tribal roles, but she asked anyway. "Why?"

"My guess? He doesn't want his problems becoming public knowledge. He's being charged with the same crime as his client. It wouldn't take long for some media-type to point out the conflict of interest. Of course, for now, only you and a handful of law enforcement officers know that."

"What are you saying?" Tanner said.

"He's telling us to go talk to Begay," Angela said.

"I'm saying, strike while the iron is hot, before Begay lawyers up again and Parker realizes he's not in as much trouble as he thinks. If you play your cards right, Begay just might sing like a canary." Sykes ducked his head back down. "Meanwhile, I'm going to try and find out if Parker has a 9mm registered in his name. I have the feeling I'm shit out of luck."

"What's in this for you?" Angela asked. She couldn't bring herself to trust Sykes. If he wanted them to talk to Begay, there had to be an angle.

Tanner sat on the edge of his desk. "Parker's too smart to use his own gun."

Sykes's head popped up again. "Agreed. So, in the spirit of cooperation, I checked on guns registered to his wife. Nothing. One thing of interest, though. Ron Henderson owned a 9mm. He kept it at his office. It was reported stolen on Monday morning, after the shootings occurred."

So that was it, thought Angela. He had found his own link to her homicide. He was going to try and take credit for solving both murders.

Tanner made a face. "He neglected to tell us about that."

Sykes grinned. "Probably didn't want to bring any more suspicion down on himself."

"Ellie Parker would have had access to Ron's gun. She could have taken it and given it to her husband."

"True, Angel, but think hard. Who else could have known about the gun?"

"Are you suggesting that Sheila Henderson took the weapon and was responsible for the shootings? You think my murder victim was a murderer."

"You're sharp." Sykes's grin expanded. "Witnesses couldn't agree on the height, but they all said the person who ran that morning was slight of build."

"That would make it premeditated," Tanner said, clearly interested in Sykes's line of thinking.

"What reason would she have for killing Smith and Begay?" Angela said.

"What can I say? She loved the birds."

"And Parker?"

"If your theory holds, he fled the scene. When she went gunning for him, he beat her to the punch, conked her over the head, and ditched the gun. End of story. Technically, he could even say he killed her in self-defense."

Angela walked it through her mind twice, and then made a face. "As far-fetched as it sounds, it's actually plausible."

"It's a work-in-progress," Sykes said, ducking back behind the monitor. "Oh, and for the record, I never told you to go see Begay."

Tanner looked at Angela. "He's not as dumb as he looks."

"I heard that, Deputy."

Tanner winked at Angela. "I say let's go talk to Begay."

Angela hesitated. She knew she should return the rattle to the evidence lockup and then call Wayne. The rattle was a museum-quality artifact, and Wayne was waiting for her back at the office to give him the word on whether or not it turned out to be the alleged murder weapon. Of course, the minute he heard that the CSI wanted corroborating evidence, her ability to maneuver on this case went out the door. There wasn't much else she could do.

"Onward," she said. "I'll drive."

Chapter 23

The guard on duty at the lockdown unit made Angela and Tanner wait. "The nurse says Prisoner Begay is in the middle of a procedure."

"What kind of procedure?" Tanner asked.

Angela figured with the new HIPAA rules there would be no information forthcoming. She was right.

"You know I can't tell you that."

"Any idea how long it will take?" she asked.

Again, the guard refused to answer except for a quick shrug of his shoulders. "I suggest you try back in fifteen."

"That's enough time to grab a cup of coffee from the cafeteria," Angela said. "I don't know about you, but I could use one."

After locating the cafeteria in the basement of Pavilion A, they sat—Angela sipping a Starbucks mocha and Tanner wolfing down a plate of meatballs and mashed potatoes. Glancing around at the modern surroundings, she couldn't help thinking that Denver Health had come a long way from the old Denver General. Curved display counters offered up everything from fruit cups to sushi, while cooking stations offered specialty foods to gourmet burgers.

Finally Angela looked back at Tanner. "I think we need a strategy."

"What, like good cop, bad cop?"

"No, just some way to convince Begay that giving up the names of his fellow worshippers—specifically Samuel Parker—is in his best interest."

"Maybe just having the douche bag bail on him will be enough."

Angela shook her head. "How about we tell him we found the murder weapon? And that, because we don't have the name of the killer, we're charging him as the accessory?"

"That would scare me."

Twenty minutes later, their bodies fortified, they arrived back at the guard station with a brainstormed approach. Angela stepped up to the guard desk.

"Is Begay free now?"

"Who?" The guard acted as if he didn't remember her, and checked her ID again. After taking more time than he needed, he picked up the receiver and dialed the nurses' station. "Visitor for Patrick Begay."

Hanging up, he shoved the sign-in clipboard toward her. She signaled for Tanner. "We're up."

"You both need to sign," said the guard. He checked Tanner's ID again, then led them over and unlocked the double doors to the unit. "This time, stop at the nurses' station."

So he did remember them.

The unit was busier than the last time they were there. Every bed was filled, including the ones in the overflow rooms. Guards were posted in front of most of the rooms and there appeared to be several doctors, nurses and aides on duty. Just as they stepped up to speak to the nurse, a contingent of doctors in medical scrubs bustled through a separate set of doors, forcing them to stand and wait.

Begay's room was visible from where they stood, but today the curtain was drawn. Angela hoped whatever type of procedure he had wouldn't prevent him from talking.

"I'll be with you in a minute," the nurse said, grabbing her stethoscope off of the desk. "We're being briefed on a patient that just came back from OR. Feel free to have a seat."

"We just need to..." then Angela was talking to air.

Turning away from the desk, she found Tanner already flopped down in one of the chairs. Angela sat down next to him.

Begay's room was hidden from view where they were seated, but they had front row seats to the drama going on in room three. Like all humans, she had a fine-tuned sense of morbid curiosity and she paid rapt attention.

Then all hell broke loose. Bells and whistles started going off. For a minute, Angela thought the patient they had just brought in had crashed. Then a nurse raced to look at the monitors above the nurses' station desk.

"Room ten," she shouted.

That was Begay's room.

One of the doctors and two nurses raced for his room. Angela started that way, when one of the guards blocked her path.

"Sit back down."

"I'm a federal officer. He's my prisoner," she said. Not exactly the truth, but close.

The guard was impassive. "Let the docs do their job."

Angela stepped to the side and tried to see what was happening.

"Code blue. Code blue."

Tanner rose and came to stand beside her. "That's not good."

Then someone in blue pushed through the medical personnel door, and the nurse who had told them to wait stepped out of Begay's room. "Stop that person."

Two of the guards and Angela sprang into action.

"Stay with Begay," she yelled to Tanner as she pushed open the door. A flash of blue to the right pulled her away from the other guards. "This way."

Racing along the corridor, she realized the guards had turned in the other direction. She was on her own. Rounding the next corner, she caught sight of the person in scrubs running. Whoever it was didn't want to be recognized. They had covered their hair with a blue cap, wore a mask, and medical booties.

She watched as the suspect slid around the next corner and hoped maybe the fact her own boots had traction would give her an edge. Then she turned the corner and came face-to-face with a hallway of medical personnel, all dressed in scrubs.

Her heart pounded in her chest from the exertion and she gulped air as she searched the crowd.

Her suspect was tall. That eliminated about half.

Her suspect had on a mask. That eliminated three-quarters.

Her suspect would try to move fast.

There! She spotted the person at the elevator, and got there just as the doors closed. The suspect had kept their face down. Damn.

Angela bolted for the stairs. She reached the first floor and scanned the crowd that had gotten off the elevator. The suspect wasn't there.

She followed suit for seven more floors. Exiting the stairwell on nine, her heart banged in her chest so hard she thought it might explode. Her legs wobbled as she walked toward the elevator, but she knew the suspect was trapped. The doors would open and there would be nowhere to go.

The elevator dinged and Angela braced for the suspect to charge.

Nothing.

She looked inside. The elevator was empty. The suspect had gotten away.

Angela backtracked to the first floor and located the security offices. Explaining the situation, she talked the woman in charge into pulling up recent footage on the security cam.

"There." Angela pointed. On the tape, the suspect could be seen exiting the elevator on the third floor and slipping through a doorway on the opposite side of the elevator. "Where does that door lead?"

"To the walkway to the garage," the security chief said.

"Do you have a camera there?"

"We have camera's everywhere." She pulled up the security footage and they watched it play out on camera. Keeping his face turned away from the camera, the suspect walked to the garage, climbed down two flights and exited onto the street.

"Can you track him?" Angela asked.

"We have cameras on the grounds only," the security chief amended. "I'm afraid we lost him."

Angela thanked the woman, and then headed back to the lockdown unit. Tanner was waiting for her by the guard station.

"Whoever it was got away," she said. "How's Begay?"

"Dead."

"What the hell happened?" Angela started for the unit doors, but Tanner grabbed her arm.

"He's gone, and they've locked the unit down tight. No one but medical personnel is allowed inside. They've posted guards at every doorway. We've been asked to submit statements in writing about what we saw."

Angela slumped into a chair in the hallway. "Did they say how he died?"

"Nothing official, but they believe the suspect pushed a syringe full of air into his PICC line. It caused an air embolism, which triggered a heart attack."

"Someone didn't want him talking," Angela said.

Tanner sat down beside her and splayed out his legs. "Care to take a guess?"

"There's no way to prove it was Sam Parker," Angela said. "I looked at the security footage. We never saw the suspect's face. All we know for sure is he was tall."

"Not good enough."

"You sound like Wayne."

"Or the CSI."

Or both. And of course, there was Sykes to face. Damn. Begay had been their last hope at pinpointing the shooter and possibly Sheila Henderson's assailant. Instead of going home with answers, they were going home in defeat.

Chapter 24

After dropping Tanner back at the Adams County Sheriff's Office, Angela tucked her tail between her legs and went back to the National Eagle Repository. Wayne had taken the news about Begay and the peyote rattle poorly. He ordered her back to work and told her let the matter drop.

She spent the rest of the afternoon catching up—documenting items that had come in during the last few days and processing requests for eagle feathers from members of Indian tribes across the country. With the United Tribes International Powwow held in Bismarck, ND, the weekend following Labor Day, and the Morongo Thunder and Lightning Powwow scheduled for late September, the requests were thicker than usual.

Traditionally, powwows were a celebration of Native American culture and heritage, and held in the spring. The number of requests they received in early-winter paid tribute to that.

In the old days, the powwows held more religious significance. If Angela remembered her history, they were a time for naming and honoring. They signified a time to welcome the new beginnings of life.

Some historians believed the word "powwow" derived from the Massachusetts Indian word "pauwau," referring to tribal and family council gatherings. The thought was that as the eastern tribes were moved west, their customs spread. But to Angela, today's powwows were different. They served more as a social gathering and carried a festive atmosphere. Indian dancers and singers, food vendors and artists traveled a "powwow circuit," most earning their livelihood during the season. The monetary payouts for coming in first in the dance and drum competitions paid in the thousands, and for most, eagle feathers were part of traditional costuming. The better the costumes, the better chance for a big payout. It was capitalism at work.

Or maybe she was just jaded.

Angela pulled the rattle out of the evidence bag and studied the markings again. She knew in her heart this was the instrument used to kill Sheila Henderson, but she couldn't tie it to the victim. The CSI confirmed it had been wiped clean—not so much as a hair or trace of fiber. The patterning matched, but without additional evidence linking that specific rattle to Sheila, Parker was about to get away with murder.

She traced her finger lightly over the intricate raised carvings. The buffalo tracks had worn over time, but the rattle itself was a superior specimen. The beadwork at the neck near the gourd and at the end showed a craftsmanship rarely equaled today. It denoted a time when it was a good day's work to toll over coiling a strand of beads onto a handle; when it was a good day's work to carve delicate bas-reliefs into wood that would span generations. Too bad two of the feathers were broken.

Angela started to place the rattle back in the peyote box, and stopped. Wait! The feathers were broken.

Setting down the rattle, she dug through the stacks of paper on her desk for the coroner's report. The pathologist who had performed the autopsy had mentioned a sticky residue on Sheila Henderson's hand that he couldn't identify. Could it have been peyote?

She finally found what she was looking for. The notation about the unidentified substance was there, but she couldn't find anywhere that it had been identified.

If the rattle had belonged to Quanah Parker, it could have been used in peyote ceremonies as early as the 1880s, staining the feathers with smoke and residue from the fires burned in the teepees. And while peyote wasn't smoked, history recorded that Quanah was treated with masticated peyote, or peyote salve, for wounds he sustained when gored by a steer—a practice he likely continued. If the CSI could match the residue on the rattle to the sticky substance on Sheila Henderson's hand, there still might be a chance of proving a connection between Sheila and Samuel Parker's peyote rattle.

Angela pulled a magnifying glass out of her desk drawer, and looked at the feathers more closely. There was enough material here that they just might be able to match it.

Reaching to set down the magnifier, the glass passed over the broken ends of the feathers and caused her to freeze.

These feathers were newly broken.

Excitement surged through her, causing her hands to tremble. What if Sheila had broken them off and that's how she'd gotten the residue on her hands? If she'd seen the blow coming and tried to deflect it, she might have grabbed hold of the feathers. If Angela could find the feather tips and match them to the feathers on the rattle, her case would be airtight.

Yeah, and then there's reality, Angela. Those feathers could be anywhere. Parker could easily have disposed of them or burned them. Even if Sheila had managed to hold onto them, the broken pieces weren't found in her car. What if she'd taken them with her when she abandoned the vehicle? If she dropped them, by now they were providing some extra insulation and cushioning for a bird's nest.

The burrowing owls!

If Sheila had the feathers in her hand when she died, there was every possibility that the burrowing owls used the feathers to line their nest. Unfortunately, the only way to find out was to open up the nest and look inside, and that constituted a violation of law—a law Angela was charged with enforcing.

Under the Migratory Bird Treaty Act, it was illegal to disturb the active nest of any migratory bird. To dig out the nest of a protected species drew heavy fines and possible jail time. In Colorado, where the burrowing owl was considered a threatened species, a person could also be charged under The Endangered Species Act, where fines climbed as high as $25K and six months imprisonment for acts of vandalism.

But these were extenuating circumstances. No one was going to arrest her or ticket her for disturbing a nest to solve a murder. And the owls weren't likely to be that upset. She had, after all, already pushed a shovel into their nest, CSI and officers had been tromping around out there for days, and the owls gave no signs of moving. It was almost as if they liked the activity and wanted to participate.

Well, they had witnessed Sheila's death. The question was, had they preserved the evidence?

Angela glanced at the time, then picked up the rattle and put it into the peyote box. CSI would be there 24/7, but the sun would be down in less than half an hour. That gave her just enough time to get out to the crime scene and check the burrow before the sun set behind the mountains. Once twilight descended on the Front Range, her chances of finding the feathers dimmed.

Locking up the repository building, Angela hurried out to her truck. Everyone else had gone home hours ago, except for the few USFW officers conducting a final sweep of the park before locking the gates at sunset. After Sheila's body was found, Wayne had ordered the stepped up patrols to ensure the park emptied out after dusk—though, as evidenced by recent events, that didn't guarantee the Refuge was empty. The last thing she wanted was to get caught rifling the nest.

Sitting in the truck and listening to the radio calls of "all clear," Angela fidgeted as the sun sank closer to the purple ridge of the Continental Divide. The window of time to work in the light was rapidly closing. When the call came across that the patrols were headed for the gate, she jammed the truck into drive and headed out.

72nd was empty as she drove out to Section 5. She didn't want to leave the truck out in the open in the event a patrol wound through a final time, so she pulled off on Chambers and tucked her vehicle into the turnaround above the bridge. Then, grabbing her windbreaker, a small spade, and a pair of gloves from behind her back seat, she headed out across the field. The quiet of the evening brought a touch of coolness to the air, while the warmth of the day still radiated off the land. The light faded in increments, casting an eerie glow on the land. She hoped the birds were still up to keeping her company.

The tape marking the western boundary of the crime scene flapped loose on the lathe, courtesy of the afternoon wind that scoured the plains day in and day out. Nearing the burrowing owls nest, she spotted one of the adults—most likely the male—standing vigil in front of the mound. Skinny legs supported a brown body, mottled white and topped with a round head. Its sun-faded wings were cupped to its sides like the arms of a soldier at attention. The bird turned his head as she moved closer. His bright yellow eyes over a pale, horn-colored beak tracked her every movement. The female, slightly darker in color, popped out of the mound to see what was happening, while four small heads fanned the opening of the hole.

Angela approached slowly. When she drew close, the male bobbed its head, screeched and hissed.

"I know," she said, wishing he could understand what was about to happen. "It's going to get worse."

Zipping up her windbreaker, she pulled on the gloves and wondered about the best way to start. A burrow was typically six to nine feet long, descending three feet and ending in a large domed chamber. If she was lucky, she would find what she was looking for in the dung piles circling the opening.

As she moved between the male and the mound, the bird swooped past her and drove his family deeper into the hole.

Angela kneeled at the entrance. She heard the sound of a rattlesnake, and hoped it was only the birds deep in the nest feigning danger. The prairie was rattlesnake country. The western diamondback rattler wasn't aggressive toward humans by nature, but it liked to hunt on summer evenings as the sun went down and it was dangerous when encountered.

The sun was dipping lower. The last rays now touched only the tops of the trees where the eagles nested. Angela pulled her flashlight from her belt, clicked it on, and propped it on the ground. The pale beam widened, shining into the mouth of the hole.

Gingerly, she reached inside and pulled a chunk from the dung ring at the edge of the burrow, then crumbled the dried excrement in her glove. Each time she came upon something different, she stopped to examine the find. She didn't want to damage the feathers in the process of unearthing them.

The feathers didn't turn up on the first pass, so she reached in and removed another chunk. Handful after handful turned up nothing except a gum wrapper and several small pieces of plastic. Scooting forward, she reached deeper into the hole. The rattling sound grew louder.

"I come in peace little birds," she said. The same thing the white man had said to the Indians.

Angela didn't have to excavate long. Her fifth handful produced the feathers she was looking for—two white tips with broken shafts.

"We're done," she said to the owls. She wasn't sure they would stay in the nest now that she had disturbed it, but she still repacked the dung, shaping it like a Jell-O mold at the front of the burrow. She would come out tomorrow to check on the birds. Often the family had a satellite burrow to move to should their home become unsafe. Unless they were threatened, the satellite served as sort of a "man-cave" for the male who spent less time at home. Angela hoped they would stay.

Sitting up, she carefully bagged the feathers and slipped them into her jacket pocket. It wasn't until she climbed to her feet that she noticed she wasn't alone.

Fear caught at her breath. Someone stood near the road, staring out into the field. Parker?

Chapter 25

Whoever it was, they weren't USFW. The car they drove looked like a newer, black SUV, but it was hard to see in the diminishing light. Tall and lean, the figure was dressed all in black, hair covered by a black knit cap, a shadow in the quickly darkening night.

"Who is it?" she called out, picking up her flashlight and shining it toward the dark figure. The beam dissipated in the night, falling short of the roadway.

No answer.

The silence made Angela edgier. Who else could it be but Parker? He must have known she would figure it out. And that after she had it was only so long before she would find what she needed to charge him with Sheila's murder. The question was, how far would he go to stop her?

Then the shadow leaned into the backseat and came up with a rifle.

Angela's breath caught in her throat. Fear stabbed her chest and a burst of adrenalin pumped through her veins.

Instinctively she reached for her weapon, as ludicrous as that was. At this distance, her 9mm Sig was no match for a rifle.

The figure leveled the gun from approximately five-hundred feet away. One and a half football fields, well in range with most hunting rifles, and this one looked like a high-powered model.

Run. The internal command rose from deep in her psyche and she bolted toward the trees. It's where her truck was, and both her phone and radio. She'd left them sitting on the console.

A shot rang out.

The bullet chipped the ground at Angela's feet and she zagged right. The second shot tore up the ground where Angela would have been standing without making adjustment. By shot number three, she was out of range.

She kept running, unable to see the ground in the dark. Her foot caught the edge of a prairie dog hole and her ankle twisted. She felt the ligaments stretch and twist, the pain sharp. She hit the ground hard and her flashlight bounced away.

On the road, a car door slammed. The engine of the SUV roared to life.

Scrambling to her feet she bolted for the tree line. The pain of each step brought tears to her eyes, but she knew she couldn't stop. At the tree line, she turned to look back. The SUV raced across the field toward her, bouncing and weaving through the prairie dog town. Within seconds, the car would be upon her.

Angela pushed deeper into the trees. The trees grew too close here to allow the shooter to follow on wheels. He would have to abandon the SUV and take after her on foot. By then, she would be at the truck and driving away.

She pushed through the grass and bushes, keeping close to the trees. A branch swept her face, scratching her skin. Her ankle caused her to run and hop.

A shot ricocheted off a nearby tree.

The USFW truck came into view and Angela ran for the vehicle. Rounding the bed of the truck, she noticed the back tires were flat. At the driver's side door, she spotted her phone and radio on the ground. Both had been smashed and broken.

Whoever was shooting at her had figured out what she was up to. The plan must have been to leave her in the field where Sheila Henderson died.

With no transportation and no way to call for help, she didn't have many options. The shooter had her pinned down in a copse of trees that stretched half a mile long and at most five-hundred feet wide on the north side of 72nd.

Another shot drove her to move, and she raced for the roost area. To cross Chambers, she would be out in the open for about twenty-five feet, but what choice did she have?

Racing for the copse of trees with her ankle swelling inside her boot, she barely noticed the pain. Bolting across the road, a bullet tore through her jacket and creased her upper arm. The burn sparked a fire of anger deep in her gut. She was not going to die out here.

If the shooter was tracking her movement through the trees and brush, sticking to the small trickle of water that constituted First Creek was the best place to stay invisible. The water soaked into her shoes, making them heavy but at the same time cooling the heat of her sprained ankle. The boot acted like a splint, and she soon found she was making better time. Her arm burned. Her right arm, her shooting arm, but she could still use it. The bullet must have only grazed her bicep.

Passing the spot where the teepee had stood, Angela moved into the thick stand of cottonwoods, willows, and hackberry bushes that bordered the north side of the clearing. She pushed deep into the trees, searching for a place to hide. With any luck, the shots had been heard by the officers locking the gate, and a rescue would ensue. If not, she was on her own.

A few feet farther, she stumbled upon a spot where a tree branch had fallen and created a natural blind. Quietly, she moved into position. A large cottonwood rose on her right, the fallen branch creating a bridge that gave her a place to prop her gun hand. The willows and hackberry had grown up around, providing natural camouflage. She forced herself to breathe shallowly and to keep still and quiet.

She could hear the shooter moving toward her through the woods, and knew she would only have one shot. Last time she was field tested with her weapon, she'd been accurate at fifty yards. If she could hold her shot until the person got within twenty-five feet or closer, there was no way she could miss.

The crackling in the bushes ricocheted in the woods, making it hard to know where the shooter was in the trees. Angela had a fairly good two hundred twenty-five degree view, but she couldn't see behind her. If her stalker went past and doubled back, Angela was dead.

To her advantage, she knew the shooter couldn't see any better than she could. Not unless he had night vision goggles.

A crack thirty feet to the left signaled the person was closing in. She held her breath and waited. Another crack. Then a dark shadow filled a gap in the trees where earlier lights from the city twinkled through.

Angela aimed and pulled the trigger.

A groan and a crash signaled she'd hit the target. Then all hell broke loose. Bullets crashed into the tree beside her, in front of her. Angela hit the ground and crawled farther away.

From her new vantage, she could see a form propped up against a tree trunk.

Another barrage of bullets forced her back to the ground. If she could somehow circle around behind, she could put an end to this.

Cautiously she moved back the way she had come, giving a wide berth to her former hiding place. She picked her way through the vegetation, flinching each time her foot caught a branch.

Angela had no way of knowing how much time had elapsed by the time she completed the circle, but the form was still there, black against the gray of the cottonwood. The gun lay on the ground, within reach, but the slump of shoulders told her it was done.

Moving quickly, she stood and pointed her gun at the back of the shooter's head. "Flinch and I'll blow your head off, Parker."

A hand moved toward the rifle, but Angela limped forward and nudged it away.

"It wasn't supposed to end this way. Why couldn't you just leave it alone?"

The voice surprised her. It wasn't a man who spoke. It wasn't Sam Parker. It was Ellie. "You?" .

"Who else?"

Angela ran the facts through her mind. Ellie had access to the 9mm that killed Smith. Ellie had access to the peyote box.

"But why?" Angela asked. "What were you trying to protect?"

"A way of life." Ellie's words slurred slightly. Angela realized she was losing blood. The woman clutched her belly and groaned. Angela moved in closer. Kicking the rifle farther away, she holstered her gun. "Do you have a phone? We need to call for help."

The phone was in Ellie's right pocket. She didn't struggle or fight when Angela took pulled it free. She didn't protest when Angela made a call to the field office and requested help.

"Stay with me, Ellie." The words sounded like they came right out of a B-movie, but the truth was, she needed to keep her talking and conscious until help arrived. "You said this was about a way of life. What did you mean?"

"He didn't care, but I did."

Angela pulled off Ellie's knit cap and handed it to her. "Press this against the wound."

"I can't," Ellie said.

"Do it!" Angela ordered, moving in closer and applying pressure to the back of Ellie's hand. She cried out in pain.

"Stop, please."

"You were saying Sam didn't care. About what?"

"His legacy. It didn't mean anything to him."

Angela thought back to their conversation at the Parker house the first day they had met. The novels on the bookshelf, the way Ellie had romanticized being the wife of a descendant of a great Indian chief.

"Tell me what happened," Angela said.

"Sam did some pro-bono work for the Native American Church. That's the first time we were exposed to the peyote ceremony. Sam thought it was foolish, detrimental to the mind. But I understood how Quanah must have felt, being cured by the healing ceremony. I thought maybe I could be cured, too."

"Of what?" Angela asked, and then remembered the picture of the small boy. "You wanted another baby."

"The doctor's said there was no reason we could never get pregnant again. Sam tested okay. The doctors pointed fingers at me, but they could never pinpoint a reason."

"So you thought if you participated in a curing ceremony...."

"That's right. I heard about the peyote ceremony that was being held out here that night from one of the wives. I asked the road man if he thought he could help."

"That's why you left Garcia's early. You didn't go home."

"Sam was working late. I told him I was going out with friends in Denver and planned to have a few drinks. He figured I'd stay over. Everything went smoothly, until the morning." Ellie moaned and she dropped her head toward her chest.

"Stay with me," Angela said, providing a shoulder for Ellie's head. "What happened in the morning?"

"Smith was still having visions. He had gone out to the bathroom and saw the bald eagle. He shot it out of the sky, then he and Begay plucked its feathers and threw its carcass onto the fire. I needed to be at work and told them we had to leave. That's when I spotted Sheila Henderson lurking about. She had a feather in her hand, and I knew she recognized me."

"What happened then?"

"I couldn't let her tell anyone what she had seen, so I grabbed the peyote rattle and followed her. Before she could get in her car, I swung it hard at her head. She dropped the feather, but managed to get in her car and drive away. When I found the wreck, I was sure she was dead."

"But why shoot Smith and Begay?"

"I told them that Sheila had seen us. They said we needed to call Sam and tell him what had happened. They were convinced Sheila's accident would be tied back to them, and they knew the fine for killing the eagle."

"You rode out there with them?"

"I had left my car in the alley behind Garcia's. I asked them to stop at my office for a minute before giving me a ride to my car."

"To steal Ron's gun." It was starting to come together. "You knew you had to kill Smith and Begay in order to keep your secret." Angela felt Ellie's head move.

"I'm married to an attorney. I knew when they found Sheila someone would figure out she'd been struck in the head. It was a way to frame Ron."

Smart, thought Angela. It kept Ellie's secret, and it made it look like Ron had killed Smith and Begay so they couldn't finger him in Sheila's death.

"You were lucky the alley cam didn't work at Garcia's."

"It never has. Sam sometimes needed footage for cases involving disputes. Everyone knew to take it into the alley."

"You were luck I didn't catch you at the hospital." Angela could hear sirens in the distance. "Did Sam know?"

Ellie emitted a sound, either a cough or a bitter laugh. "Sam submerged himself at work to bury the memories of Evan. We'd grown apart."

"Angela?" shouted a voice. Tanner. The USFW officers had called in the cavalry.

"Here!" she shouted.

It had taken Tanner a few minutes to locate Angela and Ellie, then a few more for the EMTs to stabilize Ellie for transport. The wound was severe enough that they called Flight for Life to transport her to Denver Health.

"How ironic," Angela said, as she rode in Tanner's patrol car to North Suburban Medical Center under protest. She knew her ankle was sprained, and the spot on her arm where she'd been grazed by the bullet looked more like a rug rash than anything else.

"What? That she's going to end up in the lockdown unit at Denver Health?"

"That she could end up in room ten, and then forced to leave her Indian chief, like Cynthia Parker." Angela went to put her hands in her pockets and remembered the bag with the feather tips. In all the commotion, she'd forgotten to tell anyone about finding the feathers. "Cynthia Parker lost her children, too."

"What do you have in your pocket?" Tanner asked. The deputy didn't miss much.

Angela wrestled with telling him. Now that Ellie had confessed to the crimes, there really wasn't a reason to divulge her violation of the burrowing owls' nest. But it was also the final piece of the puzzle, the nail in the coffin, and the reason she was out there tonight in the first place.

"The feathers." She told Tanner how she had figured it out. "If CSI can match the residue from Sheila's hand to the feathers, the case is ironclad."

"How did Ellie know you had figured it out? That you had a theory about the feathers."

Angela thought back. "I think she knew it the day we confiscated the peyote box. She threatened me, saying she'd sue us if there was any damage to the contents. I made her sign for the broken feathers. Without the evidence, she knew we couldn't make a case stick. It was only a matter of time."

"She almost got away with it."

Chapter26

The case went to the D.A. for prosecution, but Angela did have one thing left to do. Pulling up in front of the Henderson's house, she put the truck into park, climbed out, and retrieved a pair of crutches from the bed. The doctor had told her to stay off her foot, but he hadn't told her not to drive—a technicality, but one that worked in her favor. Her armpits were already sore, but the pain in her ankle kept her honest and off her foot.

It took her a few minutes to maneuver the steps to the front door, and before she could ring the bell, the door swung open. Leroy Henderson stood in the doorway.

"Hey," she said. "Are you here alone?"

Leroy scowled. "My dad's on his way home. I called and told him you were here."

"I just want to talk."

"I'm not supposed to talk to you anymore."

Angela pointed to the swing on the porch. "Mind if I sit?"

"Suit yourself," he said.

She hobbled over to the swing, sat and put her crutches on the deck. "Remember how I promised you we would find the person who killed your mom?"

"Yeah." Leroy inched forward, leaving the door ajar. Not unlike the burrowing owl. Curious about what was going on around him, but careful to keep open the option of diving into his burrow for safety.

"We got her."

"Her?"

Angela told him the story, skipping over a few of the details—like his father's being with Patty Litchfield the night his mom died. "Your mother was smart. She held onto the evidence that will ultimately send her killer to jail."

"That lady tried to frame my dad?"

"That's right. And she might have gotten away with it, if it hadn't been for your mom."

"And the feathers."

Angela smiled. "Yes, and a parliament of owls."

BURROWING OWLS
Athene cunicularia
Family : Strigidae

Appearance: A small ground-dwelling bird with very long legs and a small brown body with speckles of white. It has a round head without ear tufts, lemon yellow irises, bold white eyebrows and a prominent white chin strap. Its wings are rounded and its tale is short.

The male is slightly larger than the female. Still, the easiest way to tell the sexes apart is by feather color. The male spends most of his time outside of the burrow and therefore has sun-bleached plumage, compared with the darker plumage of the female, who spends most of her time inside the burrow. The owl has a life span of 6 to 8 years.

Range: There are two races of burrowing owls in North America—the Florida Burrowing Owl (floridana) and the Western Burrowing Owl (hypugaea). The Florida Burrowing Owl is restricted to Florida, the Bahamas and marginally southern Georgia; the Western Burrowing Owl ranges from east Texas, north to southern Manitoba, west across southern Canada and all across the western U.S. Common names for the burrowing owl include: Billy Owl, Prairie Dog Owl, Prairie Owl, Ground Owl and Howdy Owl.

Habitat: The burrowing owls home is a hole in the ground. They especially like holes created and then abandoned by squirrels, prairie dogs or other rodents, and even turtles. The owls are usually found in dry, level and open terrain with low vegetation and available perches. The owls like to sit on fences, utility poles, and posts or even raised rodent mounds. The abundance of mounds seems to be favored.

Voice: Its voice is a soft hollow coo-hooooo, or it can make a squeaky chuckling chatter.

Behaviors: The burrowing owl catches food with its feet and hunts by walking, hopping or running along the ground or from a perch close to its burrow. It eats primarily insects, scorpions, small mammals, birds and reptiles. The burrowing owl likes to line its nest with horse, bison or cow manure—probably to attract dung beetles, which it then captures and eats. When it feels threatened, the burrowing owl can make a sound that imitates a rattlesnake in order to scare predators away.

Conservation: The populations of burrowing owls are decreasing and it appears on the endangered or threatened lists in many states. The primary source of mortality is collision with cars, with human activity increasing on the species range due to land development and oil and gas development.

Christine Goff's *Birdwatcher's Mystery* Series

A Rant of Ravens

In an attempt to escape a hellish marriage, Rachel Stanhope retreats to her Aunt Miriam's ranch in Colorado. As a favour to her bird-loving aunt, Rachel agrees to host meetings of the local bird watching society. But on her first birding expedition to find a Le Conte's sparrow, she makes a much more disturbing discovery: the body of a journalist investigating a local bird trafficking scheme. Now sweet Aunt Miriam is the prime suspect, and it's up to Rachel to solve the murder mystery.

Death of a Songbird

In desperate need of respite, Lark Drummond accompanies her friend, Rachel Stanhope, on a birding expedition. But their relaxing afternoon takes a gruesome turn when Lark witnesses her business partner's malevolent murder through her spotting scope. With the help of their birdwatching club, she sets out to solve the tortuously complex mystery. However, as more clues surface—and disappear—it soon becomes apparent that this case is much more menacing and dangerous than they'd originally bargained for.

A Nest in the Ashes

Eric Linenger's job, as a National Park Service ranger, isn't always easy. He is tasked to oversee a "prescribed burn" of a thousand acres in Rocky Mountain National Park, which not only means containing the fire to the necessary acreage, but also protecting the precious habitats of the local birds. However, once the fire is ablaze, the delinquent flames spread wildly out of control, and Eric's boss, Wayne Devlin, is found dead near the fire's origin. Eric takes it upon himself to investigate an increasingly perplexing arsonist mystery, and uncovers the disturbing truth that many people, including his own friends, had the motivation to ensure the deadly fire would rage unchecked.

Death Takes a Gander

Bad luck seems to follow U.S. Fish and Wildlife Special Agent, Angela Dimato. Her partner is dead, and all evidence points to a mere accident as the cause. And when she is assigned to oversee a local fishing tournament, she discovers two hundred dead Canada Geese. Following her famed intuition, Angela investigates—with the help of an eccentric group of birdwatchers. Startlingly, she discovers that her partner's death may be connected, and may not have been so freakishly accidental after all.

A Sacrifice of Buntings

Rachel Wilder's world takes a whirlwind turn when renowned bird researcher Guy Saxby falls in love with her friend, Dorothy MacBean. Even more shocking is when Guy's protégé is mysteriously murdered and Guy is the chief suspect. As Rachel and Dorothy work hard to clear his name, Rachel discovers the victim's innovative exposé on the Painted Bunting, upstaging his own mentor's research. Just how far would someone go to avoid this?

A Parliament of Owls

Angela Dimato, a tenacious U.S. Fish and Wildlife Agent, struggles to rebuild her life after the murder of her partner. During a routine tour of the Rocky Mountain Arsenal, Angela assesses the growing prairie dog town within the wildlife refuge when, to her horror, she discovers the body of a soccer mom sprawled out among the burrows. With her trademark instinct and her gun in tow, Angela investigates the murder, even as she battles the crippling flashbacks haunting her from her partner's case. The investigation takes a sinister turn when the dead woman is identified as the leader of a group petitioning for the eradication of the prairie dog town. As Angela digs toward the truth, she finds her only hope is to tap into the wisdom of the case's sole eye witness—a burrowing owl—before more lives become at stake.